Raves for N

Admission of Love

"A well-crafted story."
—*Affaire de Coeur,* 4½ stars

Three Times a Lady

"This sneaky little romance heats up gradually, then sizzles until done."
—Doubleday's Black Expression Book Club review

Heavenly Match

"*Heavenly Match* is a wonderfully romantic story with an air of mystery and suspense that draws the reader in, encouraging them to put aside everything and everyone until they have read the book in its entirety."
—*Rawsistaz* review, 4 stars

Can't Get Next to You

"'Sexy as sin' describes this provocative novel to a T."
—*Romantic Times BOOKclub,* 4½ stars, Top Pick

Let's Do It Again

"Run to the bookstore and pick up this delightful read. This reunion story is touching, warm, sensuous, and at times sad. But just try to put Bryant's book down."
—*Romantic Times BOOKclub,* 4½ stars, Top Pick

Books by Niobia Bryant

Admission of Love
Three Times a Lady
Heavenly Match
Can't Get Next to You
Let's Do It Again

ANTHOLOGIES

You Never Know
"Could It Be?"

NIOBIA BRYANT

Count on This

ISBN-13: 978-1-58314-648-4
ISBN-10: 1-58314-648-2

COUNT ON THIS

www.kimanipress.com

Printed in U.S.A.

This is dedicated to the artists whose music plays softly in the background as I am shut in my office banging away at the computer keys:

Mary J. Blige
Keyshia Cole
Lauryn Hill
Kanye West
Jay-Z
Usher
Alicia Keys

Just to name a few…

Prologue

Surprise, Surprise

Gabrielle "Gabby" Bennett flew down the spiral staircase with the agility and speed of a track star. Excitement was her fuel. She barely screeched to a halt in the foyer to fling open the door with a smile as big as could be. "Ape," she exclaimed with obvious pleasure as she stepped forward to pull her sister into a tight embrace.

The feel of her sister's arms encircling her, as well, felt good. Damn good. It had only been a week since she'd left for a brief holiday, but Gabby had missed her like crazy. They were close. As close as two sisters could be.

The physical distance between them was no comparison to their emotional closeness, but Gabby had been thrilled when she'd finally convinced Ape to move to Richmond and live in the guest house on the estate. April had taken over Gabrielle's old position as Maxwell's assistant so that Gabby was able to travel with her husband and spend more time with the baby. Ape was her sister, her best friend and her reality check when needed.

In fact, it had been her sister who had helped turn her from a duckling to a swan and helped her catch her man—the love of her life—Maxwell Bennett.

"When did you get back? Did you have fun? Why do you have your luggage? Haven't you been home?"

April Dutton dropped her leather suitcase by the door. "Dang, Gabby, you got more questions than Oprah," she teased, bumping her shapely hip against her taller sister as she moved to the kitchen. "Where's my nephew?"

Gabrielle followed her. "Addie's putting him down for a nap up—"

A ring tone—50 Cent's "Disco Inferno"—sounded from the back pocket of April's jeans. She pulled it out, looked at it briefly and then set it on the large island in the center of the French-country kitchen. "I have first dibs on kissing and sniffing his neck when he wakes. Aunt's privilege and all that," she said, smiling, although it didn't quite reach her normally bright and chipper eyes.

Gabrielle noted the still-ringing phone and then shifted her gaze to her sibling. "He's getting bigger every day."

"If he eats like that husband of yours I can imagine," April said dryly as she moved to the fridge.

Gabrielle crossed her arms over her chest, leaning her shapely hip against the island as she studied her sister. Ape wasn't being Ape. Not quite sassy enough. Not at all cocky and bold enough. Her constant smile wasn't in place the way it usually was. She seemed distracted, and there was an obvious wrinkle between her shaped brows.

Something was up.

"April, is something wrong?"

The cell phone sounded again.

April drank her juice and slowly sashayed to

the island to pick up the cell phone, looked at it very casually, and then sat it back down with a suck of her teeth.

"Sweet Jesus, Ape. Who…is…that?" Gabrielle asked, exasperated.

Ape laughed a little—very cynical and short—as she looked at her sister. "My husband," she answered simply with a tinge of defiance in her tone.

"Your…what?" Gabrielle roared as the phone sounded yet again.

Chapter 1

Viva Las Vegas

"Excuse me."

April "Ape" Dutton didn't look up from the cell phone as she stepped aside from standing in the elevator's entrance to allow someone to step inside with her. The subtle, all-too-warm-and-sexy scent of a man's cologne surrounded her like a fine mist. She inhaled it deeply and released a soft little grunt indicative of her pleasure.

She looked up at the other occupant of the elevator. Her heart double pumped at the chiseled profile of the man standing beside her. Like a connoisseur, she let her gaze travel from the tip of his head down to his size-twelve feet—a guess.

He was handsome. Wildly so. Almost exotic. The kind of Denzel, Boris or Blair type of handsome that made a woman pause. Stare. Desire.

Light, café-au-lait complexion. Strong jaw. Deep blue-green eyes. Soft, full, kissable lips. The kind of high cheekbones African warriors were born with. Angular features. Soft jet-black hair. A trimmed mustache and goatee. Slender-yet-strong build most men dreamed of having.

Although April generally favored men with skin as deep, dark and sweet as molasses, this man had the fair complexion of Terrence Howard and the blue-green eyes of Michael Ealy from *Barbershop*. But what piqued her interest was the cut of his navy suit and the casual elegance with which he stood with one of his hands in the pocket of his pants. Only a blind woman wouldn't think that this man, his total package, was *i-t* it.

The elevator slowed to a stop at the lobby.

Just as the doors slid open, he turned his head and looked down at her with a smile—a devilish and disarming smile.

April knew there was so much behind that smile. Maybe a little cockiness. Even arrogance. She knew a man like him was used to women giving him all the attention he ever wanted or needed.

"Ladies first," he said, bowing his head a bit and waving his arm toward the open elevator doors.

Somehow all of the classic April moves left her. No slick lick of the lips. No flutter of her long, lush lashes. Not even an extra wiggle of her ample buttocks and hips as she strode out of the elevator with a soft, "Thank you."

When she happened to look back over her shoulder, he was gone.

"Oh, well," she sighed, even though she felt a little let down.

She was in Las Vegas and this was a town of no regrets.

She turned in a slow circle and looked at her surroundings. The lobby of the Bellagio Hotel was spectacular. The luxury and splendor was a far cry from the little two-bedroom apartment she had when she lived in Savannah,

Georgia. Yet somehow in the midst of the bright lights and fast pace of Vegas, the hotel was calm and serene, elegant and tasteful—adjectives usually not associated with Sin City. It was like nothing April had seen before.

Her cell phone began to vibrate in her hand.

"Talk to me," she said into the phone.

"Are you still getting dressed? I'm starving."

April's round face broke into an instant smile at the sound of her best friend, Clayton Wilkes. "Where are you?" she asked.

"In the lobby."

"*I'm* in the lobby."

April turned left and then right, walking forward a bit as she searched for him.

"I'm right behind you, Ape."

She whirled and saw Clayton strolling up to her, closing his cell phone to slide it into the pocket of his tailored linen shorts.

Hands-down he was one of the most beautiful men God ever created. The man was ridiculously handsome. Unblemished mocha complexion. Groomed beard. Close-shaven hair that was jet-black, thick and fine.

As always he was impeccably dressed. Today he wore a white silk T-shirt and linen shorts that perfectly fitted his tall, muscular frame.

He alone could wear linen in Vegas heat and not have one blessed wrinkle.

April had wanted every inch of his divineness from that first day she moved into her new apartment complex and saw him lounging by the community pool in a bikini that rode far too low on his narrow hips and clung far too close to his endowment. And she'd been determined to have him—pulling some rather risque stunts to get his attention—until he told her in no uncertain terms that he was gay.

April was not a "fag hag" by any means. Clayton was not the stereotypical two snaps up and "I'll cut you" homosexual man. He was masculine. Manly. Hard. No arched eyebrows. No juicy clear lip gloss, clear nail polish or processed hair. He didn't bandy around "girlfriend" and talk in feminine tones.

He could easily live life on the down-low without a sistah having a clue, but he was gay and proud.

Now they were the best of friends and even laughed at the little stunts she used to pull to get his attention, like the time she locked herself out of her apartment in a negligee—on purpose—and then knocked on his door hoping he would ravish her. They were so close that after several weekend visits to see her in Richmond, Clayton made the move there himself, purchasing a modest three-bedroom home just twenty-five minutes from Maxwell's estate.

Clayton gave the usual once-over to the strapless white dress she wore. "Nice dress. Wrong shoes."

April looked down at her straw espadrilles—which she loved. "What's wrong with my shoes?" she asked.

His mouth opened.

April held up her hand. "Forget it. Don't wanna know and sure don't care."

He laughed.

Arm in arm they made their way to the hotel's twenty-four hour restaurant, Café Bellagio. April immediately felt at peace in the beautiful surroundings of the botanical garden and conservatory. It was certainly like no café she had seen.

"Have I thanked you enough for bringing me on this trip?" April asked as Clayton seated her.

"Yup," he said, taking his own seat across from her.

"Well thank-you is one thing you can't get enough of."

Clayton smiled at her.

One month ago, he'd bought a fifty dollar

raffle ticket on a week-long trip to Las Vegas for two. He won and asked April to accompany him. Thank the heavens she worked for Max because all she had to say was the word and he gave her the time off.

Their waiter, Raoul, was a handsome specimen, and April didn't miss the way Clayton's eyes followed the slender man as he walked away to put in their orders.

"You know if either of us gets *lucky,* outside of gambling, then he—"

"Or she," Clayton added, reluctantly turning those eyes on her.

"Right." April lifted her glass of ice water and lemon. "He or she should not feel the need to babysit the other. Deal?"

Raoul walked past their table. Clayton looked up at him.

April smiled at Raoul's double take when he caught Clayton's intense gaze on him. His customary "I'm here to serve you" grin went to a *whole* 'nother level.

"Deal," Clayton answered without breaking his stare from Raoul's as the man moved on to the rear of the restaurant.

She smiled into her glass. "Maybe you two should get a room," she drawled.

"Be right back." Clayton rose and moved in Raoul's direction.

April's phone rang and she retrieved it from her purse. At the sight of Tyrone's number, she sent the call straight to voice mail. *Please.* Tyrone was her recent ex. He was the ultimate everything in the bedroom—he had the skill to make her talk in tongues—but his game outside of the bedroom was weaker than sugar water compared to Kool-Aid. After nearly a year of good sex and little else she had finally kicked the muscle-head to the curb with a pointy-toe boot.

She was just dropping the phone back into her ornate leather hobo purse when Clayton walked over pushing a slip of paper into his wallet and then slipping the wallet into his pocket before he took his seat.

"Success?" she asked.

Clayton winked. "And you know it. "

"After breakfast I'm on the way to the spa, dahling," she said in an exaggerated, haughty tone. "There's a coconut scrub and stone massage with my name all over it."

"Raoul actually offered to take us sightseeing. He gets off in thirty minutes."

"Then hopefully you'll be getting off in forty-five minutes," April teased.

Clayton gave her a deadpan expression. "Shut up."

"Oh, no. I'm not playing third wheel. We'll part ways and just meet up for dinner. We have eight-o'clock reservations at Le Cirque. Cool?"

"Cool."

After breakfast April and Clayton did part ways. She headed for the spa for her ten-o'clock appointment.

She had just breezed past a doorman holding the door open for her when she froze. The scent of cologne—*his* cologne—teased her senses. Her nipples tightened into tight buds and her pulse raced a bit. April turned and found him talking to a bellhop outside the hotel.

Her eyes locked on the devilishly handsome man from the elevator.

He smiled and laughed at something the bellhop said before the bellhop walked back into the hotel, and returned moments later holding open one of the glass doors. Six brothas in varying levels of attractiveness all walked out of the hotel with raucous laughter. Mr. Beautiful and the fellas—obviously his crew—followed the bellhop to a black stretch Hummer limousine that pulled up to the curb.

One by one the men climbed in.

Turn around, April willed him silently, only wanting another look at him. *Turn the hell around.*

Mr. Beautiful was just about to climb into the Hummer when he did just that. He turned. And his eyes—those incredible bluish green eyes—locked on April.

He smiled at her in recognition before turning back and climbing into the vehicle with his friends.

April smiled in return, but he was already gone. That made her feel incredibly stupid. *Real cool, Ape. Real cool.* She rolled her eyes at her own foolishness for gawking behind a man, as she turned and strolled into the Spa Bellagio.

Alexander "Lex" Macmillan nursed his beer under the dim lights of one of the sky boxes at the Sapphire, one of the largest strip clubs in Vegas.

Lex couldn't wait to get back to his penthouse suite at the Bellagio and get away from the frat-boy atmosphere. He enjoyed a good time like the next man, but the weekend-long bachelor party in Sin City was draining him, and they were only on day two.

Next Saturday his best friend, Warrick "War" Kinsey, was marrying the woman of his dreams, Elizabeth Cannon. It had been the suggestion of their mutual friend, Derrick Lyles, to jet War away for the ultimate bachelor party.

With strip clubs open twenty-four hours a day it had been a round of T & A ever since they arrived last night. Lex had seen enough breasts and buttocks to last him a lifetime. Real ones. Fake ones. Small ones. Big ones. Loose ones. Firm ones.

The constant lights. The constant motion. The constant action and activity. Vegas.

"Go, War. Go, War."

Lex turned his head and then shook it as he watched four topless dancers lead War to a chair in the center of the skybox. One by one they took turns giving him a lap dance to top all lap dances as the rest of the fellas formed a semicircle around the spectacle. Lex looked on with amusement from a distance as the next woman straddled War and began to make every ounce of her body vibrate—probably even her toes. Lex had to admit the move was...impressive.

"I still can't believe War's letting Elizabeth chain him down." Derrick said, sitting down beside Lex with a bottle of beer in his hand. Derrick was the ultimate bachelor. A stereotypical man's man. Sexually adventurous. Refused to be tied down to one woman. More girlfriends than days in the week. Brash. Bold. Explicit.

"It's just marriage, Lyles, not a death sentence."

Derrick cut his eyes at Lex as he took a swig of his beer.

"I don't see you running to the altar."

Lex shrugged. "I'm not running away from it, either."

"I am. Matter of fact, when it comes to the altar I'm running away faster than Jesse Owens, Carl Lewis, and Flo-Jo combined. Believe that, dawg."

The men laughed together.

"What's Daniels up to?" Lex asked as he set his empty beer bottle on the table.

"Marcus and Meesha are in Greece for the month. Her grip on my dawg's nuts is tighter than a pit bull's bite."

Lex shook his head, thinking of Derrick's business partner and best friend, Marcus Daniels. The men owned MDDL, a bicoastal entertainment law firm/sports agency. But that's where the similarities ended. Marcus was sedate, calm, the quintessential family man, and Derrick was...Derrick.

Lex felt he was somewhere between the two men when it came to women and relationships.

"Love is gonna knock you flat on your ass, Lyles."

"Not a chance."

Lex watched as his friend walked away and whispered something in the ear of one of the dancers who had more curves than a letter *S*. Seconds later she was pushing Derrick into a chair and working hard for her money.

He was glad when the two-hour rental of the skybox wound to an end. He was hungry and not in the mood to have his food fried or barbecued or drenched in hot sauce and served up with more T & A and smiles.

Lex didn't consider himself a snob by any means but he preferred lobster and filet mignon to buffalo wings anyday.

The sun had set and it was a Vegas night when they emerged from the club. Cars zoomed up and down the strip. The street and the buildings lining the street were lit up like Christmas.

Lex was just climbing into the limo with his friends when he heard Derrick instruct their driver to take them to yet another strip club. Count me out. "Um, I'm gonna head back to the hotel," he said, stepping back down onto the sidewalk.

War looked disappointed. "Come on, Lex, don't bail on me now," he said.

"I'll hook up with y'all later."

"Well hop in. We'll drop you to the hotel," Derrick offered, already popping the cork on a new bottle of Dom.

Under normal circumstances Lex would gladly accept a ride from his friends. But he knew that his friends could be a little juvenile when in a group and drinking. As soon as he got into that limo, they would lock the doors and not open them until the limo arrived at the next strip club.

He wasn't falling for it.

"Have fun." Lex shut the door and stepped back onto the curb.

As soon as the limo pulled away, he signaled for a cab, and luck was on his side. "The Bellagio, please," he said, climbing in and shutting the door.

In the dim interior he checked the time on his Smartphone. It was just after seven. He would go back to his penthouse suite, wash away the scents of smoke and the dancers' clinging body oils, maybe have an in-room massage and order room service.

He'd rejoin the bachelor party tomorrow. Tonight? Tonight was his. And he deserved it.

One year ago his father, Harris "Big Mac" Macmillan, stepped down as CEO of Macmillan, Inc., one of the top advertising firms in the country. And at twenty-nine, the position, and all the responsibilities and expectations that come along with it, had become his. That meant working nearly nonstop to maintain the brilliant legacy his grandfather began and his father continued.

Once in the foyer of his suite, Lex turned off his cell phone and stripped down nude as he strode into the elaborately decorated living room and dining room through to the bedroom. He moved with strength, every muscle flexing—a testament to the stringent workout regime he used to have time for. Soon his rigid abdomen would soften from an eight-pack to a four-pack because he couldn't remember the last time he made time to work out.

Lex enjoyed a long steamy shower. By the end of it he decided to pass on both the massage and room service. He wanted to enjoy a meal at a nice restaurant and if he had to do it alone he was confident enough to do just that.

Back in New York, even Lex's personal life had been put on the back burner for work. He wasn't a monk by any means, but lately his sex life was more like wham-bam than wining and dining. To be honest, his phone was filled with the names and numbers of plenty of willing women, but not one had lit that kind of fire and desire in him to keep him away from work.

Once dressed, Lex slid his wallet into his pocket and walked out of the suite's foyer into the lobby. He glanced down at his Jaeger-LeCoultre watch just as the elevator doors slid open and he stepped inside.

As the doors closed, Lex called the concierge for the number to make a reservation at Le Cirque. The elevator slowed to a stop at the twenty-eighth floor just as the concierge connected him to the restaurant.

The doors slid open.

Lex looked up just as the same beautiful woman he saw on the elevator earlier stepped inside. She paused a little at the sight of him and he knew she recognized him as well. His heart pounded.

"How you doing?" he asked, moving the phone from his mouth a bit.

She smiled as she stepped in beside him and turned to face the closing doors. "Fine and you?"

"I'm good."

"That's good."

"Yes, I'd like a reservation for one—" He felt her eyes shift up to him.

"For one?" the hostess asked.

Lex frowned. "Yes, for one," he stressed with plenty of attitude.

"I'm sorry, sir. We're booked until 9:30."

Lex glanced at his watch again. It was only eight o'clock. He'd just have to eat somewhere else. "No, thank you." The elevator slowed to a stop and she smiled at him as she walked off. Lex let his eyes take in her shapely full frame, loving the way the flared skirt of the strapless black dress she wore swished against her buttocks ending above shapely legs with thick calves.

He stepped off the elevator, his dinner reservation forgotten as he slipped his hand into his pocket and watched her walk away. Sexy. Confident. And somehow—without even trying—naughty. So naughty that he wanted to know what was under her skirt. A Brazilian wax and some sheer bikinis? Maybe a thong?

He grinned at that thought.

She turned suddenly, the dress raising slightly like a parasol. He dropped the grin before she thought he was silly. She started back toward him and he enjoyed that view as well.

She was just as enticing coming as she was going. Her hair was soft, straight, and jet-black with a soft part that sent the hair down the sides of her pretty, round cinnamon face. And what a beautiful face it was: slanted eyes that gave her an exotic flare; high cheekbones, a brilliant dimpled smile above a soft rounded chin.

She came to a stop before him.

"I have a reservation for two at Le Cirque, and my best friend has made other plans with a sexy waiter named Raoul. Care to join me for dinner?"

Lex liked her style. In fact at that moment there wasn't a thing he didn't like about her. "Lex Macmillan." He offered her his hand.

She slid her hand into his with ease. "April Dutton."

His whole body tingled from her simple touch.

Chapter 2

As We Lay

"Here's to good wine, good food and good company."

April smiled at his toast, raising her glass to lightly tap against his as they sat beneath the colorful, swooping, silk-tented ceilings of the circus-themed French restaurant. "Here, here."

She could hardly believe she was sitting across from Mr. Beautiful. Clayton canceling their dinner plans at the last minute was now a moot point. Because of his tryst with Raoul, she was sitting across from a man who made her entire body feel alive.

"This is one of my favorite restaurants. Too bad they don't have one in New York," he said, taking a bite of his lamb.

"You're from the city that never sleeps, huh?" April took small bites of her scallops, even though she wanted to tear into her meal as if she were home alone. She could eat a man under the table.

"Yes, and most of the time I'm so busy working *I* never sleep."

"All work and no play will make Lex a dull boy." April flipped her hair over her shoulder, giving Lex her flirtiest smile. He was so different from any man she'd known. Serious. Comfortable in his sexiness but not conceited. Focused. Refined. Intelligent. Cool. Knowledgeable. Well rounded. Suave. She could go on forever. "What exactly do you do?"

He looked at her with those intense eyes. "I work in advertising," he said, sounding vague.

"Well, don't be so busy helping other people get rich that you let your own life pass you by, Lex." She winked at him. "Just my opinion."

"What about you? Tell me about you." He

leaned back in his chair and watched her, his long fingers lightly rubbing the rim of his wine-glass.

"Not much really," she said, setting her elbows on the table as she leaned forward. "Well for the first time since I was sixteen I'm in between jobs. I used to live in Savannah but I quit my sucky job as a clerk for the county. I moved to Richmond with my sister, Gabby, and her husband, Maxwell Bennett, once they had my nephew."

"Maxwell Bennett the artist?"

"That's him," she answered with pride.

He looked impressed. "We have several of his originals at the offices."

It was her turn to be impressed. "So hard work does pay because it would take my whole old salary and a long-ass payment plan to buy one."

Lex laughed—full, rich and deep.

April stared at him, thinking he looked even better with his face open and alive with laughter. "You should laugh and smile more often," she told him, setting her chin in her hand.

He looked reflective for a moment. "I should surround myself with people who make me smile and laugh more often."

April picked up her wineglass by the stem and raised it slightly with a lick of her glossy lips. "Here's to new friends and lots of laughter."

Lex raised his glass, as well. "Here, here."

"Four!"

Lex smiled at the roulette dealer's exclamation as he added Lex's winnings to the pile of chips he had sitting on the four spot of the table. April grabbed his shoulders and whirled him around to jump up and fling her arms around his strong neck. He placed one arm around her waist.

"I told you this was fun," she whispered in excited tones near his ear as she patted his back.

A shiver of pure awareness shimmied over his body.

Lex wasn't a gambling man. He believed in sure things. Not odds or games of chance. He believed money was better served. He believed it wasn't fun to walk the thin line between winning money and losing it.

Until he met April.

She was invigorating. Alive. Fun. Carefree. Spontaneous.

Everything he wasn't.

"All bets down."

He reluctantly released her as he picked up his winnings. He had doubled his five-hundred-dollar bet and had walked the line enough for one night.

"You're not betting again?" she asked as the dealer changed out someone's hundred-dollar bill.

He placed a fifty-dollar chip in her hand. "Bet for me," he requested, sliding his hands into the pockets of the tailored black slacks of his suit.

April bumped her hip against his. "Let's bet on today," she said, placing the chip on twenty-four.

The dealer took final bets and then spun the wheel.

He stepped behind her, his eyes on the wheel until he felt her eyes on him. She was looking over her bare shoulder. He returned her gaze with question.

"You're really handsome in all black," she said huskily, her eyes clouding.

That one smouldering look made his penis harden in an instant. *Wow.* "So do you," he returned, his eyes squinting a bit as she boldly continued their heated stare.

"Six!" The dealer exclaimed.

"Damn. And I thought today was lucky," she said softly, never once turning back to the table.

Her face was sweet and sexy, playful and serious...all at once. He followed an impulse to stroke her chin. "I don't know. It's feeling pretty damn lucky for me."

"Damn brotha, are you real?" she asked, slightly playful as they moved away from the table and she pinched herself.

Lex laughed as they walked out of the casino. His phone rang, and he slid it out of the inside pocket of his suit jacket to look at.

"Your buddies still looking for you?" she asked.

Lex nodded, sliding the phone back into the pocket. "I'll catch up with them tomorrow."

"Is it my *fabulous* company you want to be in or theirs you're trying to avoid?"

"Both."

"Good answer."

"You don't have a girlfriend back home who would care that I'm this close to you during a beautiful gondola ride?" April's body was still waiting for his answer.

Lex tightened his hold around her shoulders, her body warmly encased in his suit jacket. "If I had a girlfriend I wouldn't have accepted your invite to dinner nor would I have brought you on a romantic gondola ride."

She relaxed back against his hard chest. "Well let me thank you for keeping me company this evening, especially with my best friend off enjoying his own little taste of Vegas."

Lex stiffened. "His?"

April nodded, her hand lightly resting atop his where it sat on her shapely hip. "Yes."

"I thought you said your best friend was with a waiter named Raoul."

"Yeah, I did."

"Oh…okay."

April just smiled. "Get it?"

"Got it."

"Good."

They fell silent as the gondolier steered them along the large lagoon made to look like an authentic Venetian canal. The water's light lapping sound against the boat was soothing, and completely in contrast to the Vegas strip upon which the Venetian resort sat.

"You're really a nice guy," April offered, as the gondolier began to softly serenade them. "The nicest guy I've met in a long time. Even thought we're different as night and day—"

"I don't think we're that different," Lex offered.

April sat up from his chest and turned to look at him. "Puh-leeze. You're a sophisticated New Yorker and I'm the little country girl used to working for thirteen bucks an hour. I've never ever eaten at a restaurant like Le Cirque before or stayed in a hotel this beautiful and expensive. My best friend won a contest or I couldn't have ever afforded the Bellagio. And I know this is as close to Venice as I'll ever get. Trust me."

"How can you be so sure this isn't my first time for this, as well?"

April arched a brow. "The fact that you used 'as well' is a big red flag, for one."

Lex just laughed.

"For two, the fact that you are accustomed to nice things is written all over you. I'm not judging. I'm just being real."

"If I am accustomed to nice things does this mean I'm better than someone who isn't?" he asked, pulling her back against his chest with one strong arm.

April settled back against him with a sigh. "No, I don't buy into the class thing. I'm just saying that even if I lived in New York, you and

I would probably never cross paths, and I would never know what a great guy you were. So I'm just enjoying tonight and seeing it for what it is...one night."

"Hey."

April tilted her head back to look up at him, the space between their mouths intimate. Close. Teasing. Taunting. "Yes?"

"I'm not ready for tonight to end," he whispered, his breath lightly fanning against her lips.

April turned fully and raised her hand to stroke his cheek. Electricity crackled between them. Chemistry couldn't be denied. Passion was there simmering and ready for the heat to be turned up.

"Me either," she answered, raising her chin to his with clear intent.

As soon as the elevator door closed behind them, Lex pulled April into his arms, lifting her until she was able to wrap her thick shapely legs around his waist.

She lightly clutched his head as Lex stepped forward and pressed April's back to the elevator wall, his hands rising to caress her thighs deeply as they kissed with a fierceness that was wild, erratic, untamed.

April cried out hoarsely as Lex kissed a trail down her neck and then suckled the soft flesh above her strapless top as he ground his hard penis against her. "God, that feels *sooooo* good," she moaned, biting her bottom lip.

"The elevator isn't moving," he whispered against her cleavage.

April laughed a little. "Guess we were a little busy." She kissed him again. Hard and hot. "I'm on the twenty-eighth floor."

Lex leaned back to meet her eyes, his breathing ragged and his heart pounding. "I have the penthouse suite."

April's chest heaved with her own heated breathing as she arched a brow. "Your room it is."

They barely made it inside the dark foyer of Lex's penthouse suite before they stripped each other with trembling fingers and nagging teeth. Naked and heated. Their hands glided and groped, stroked and caressed the contours of each other's body as he pressed her body down against the shockingly cold marble of the foyer's floor.

April gasped from the naughty, erotic sandwich created with his heat and the floor's coldness. "Yes, suck my titties. Suck 'em," she demanded hoarsely, her hand pressed against the softness of his fine hair as his lips sought and found her thick aching nipples.

The first feel of his tongue flickering around her areola before he suckled the nipple into his eager mouth made April cry out in passion. "Yes, yes, yes," she whispered huskily.

Her cries hardened him even more, and he tried his best to draw nearly all of her hot breast into his mouth as he circled his narrow hips—each move causing his penis to be stroked by the softness of her belly. He wanted to come, but he wanted to make sure she would come even more.

With one last gentle tug of her nipple in his teeth, Lex shifted his head to her other breast, loving the feel of the plush, velvet-soft flesh against his mouth.

April moved her hands down to tightly grasp his hard, square buttocks before she slapped each one lightly. Lex grunted in pleasure, and she smacked him lightly again. "Oh, you like that, huh?"

She felt him nod against her breast and she rubbed his buttocks before she smacked them yet again, feeling decidedly naughty. She didn't care. She just wanted to enjoy tonight.

To enjoy him. To make a memory she would never forget once he was gone from her life and to create a memory he would never forget, either. She wanted him to quiver whenever he thought of her and to want her even when he knew they would never see each other again.

Lex rose and settled on his knees, straddling her. "Roll over, April," he demanded huskily, his hands constantly touching, stroking, caressing her body.

She did as he bade.

His hands massaged her thick thighs and her firm buttocks. He bit his tongue as he used one hand to lightly tap his erection against her buttocks making a slight echoing noise in the quiet of the suite. From left to right. Right to left. *Bap...bap...bap.*

"Feel good?" he asked thickly.

The side of her face was pressed to the cold floor as she nodded and wiggled her bottom, arching it higher for him. "Do it again."

Bap.

"Harder," she begged with no shame, her thighs pressing the lips of her vagina closed. The friction teasing the swollen, aching and moist bud folded within the thick lips.

Bap!

Lex felt her tremble, and he had to fight not to bury himself deep within her. He moved away from her and she murmured in regret. He rose to flood the foyer with light. He stood there for a moment, his erection hanging awkwardly from his body, as he enjoyed the sight of April's voluptuous curves. Her softly rounded shoulders. The sexy small of her back. The two dimples at the top of each glorious buttock. And her legs. Thick, shapely and sturdy legs.

Just simply sexy.

He retrieved protection from his wallet, flinging the pants back to the floor as he sheathed himself with a studded and lubricated condom that figuratively had her name written all over it.

Squatting, he picked her up into his arms with ease and carried her through the suite into the master bedroom.

April clung to him, her hands playing in the soft hairs at his nape.

Lex lay April on the bed and pressed one knee in the plushness to join her, but she rolled out of the way. "My turn," she told him with sexy confidence as she used one finger pressed to his hairless, muscled chest to push him down onto his back.

April sat on her knees beside him. "Nice view," she said with a wicked smile as she perused his flat abdomen, hard chest and chiseled thighs. His penis was thick and long, and darker than the rest of him. The brotha was bad from the top of his head to his feet.

Lex put his hands behind his head and observed her full breasts, slightly pudgy, but sexy, stomach and the smooth, bald mound between her thighs. That made him swallow hard over a lump in his throat. "Same here."

She smiled as she straddled him backward, squatting above him with ease as she used one hand to guide her core down onto his hardness. Her lips welcomed him, suckled him and coddled him as she moved downward with deliberate slowness until all of him filled her. They both tensed. The air in the room was electrified, seeming to crackle about them like static.

April flung her head back, her eyes closed as she felt him throb inside her.

Lex bit his bottom lip, his eyes transfixed on the sight of her plush buttocks pressed against his abdomen as her walls held his penis like a tight fist. He brought his hands up to lightly grasp her waist as April began to slowly and rhythmically ride him in a snakelike motion. The combined effect of the feel of her tight and rigid walls gripping and then releasing his tool as she slid up and down the length of him with ease had him shivering. Breathless. Anxious.

She reached down to wrap her hand around each of his ankles. Her moans floated to the ceiling. Her heart raged. Her body soared.

Fixated, he watched the snakelike motion of her hips and the gentle shake of her buttocks as she popped her hips. "Shit," he swore, perspiration coating his muscled frame as he watched his penis disappear and then reappear with each hot glide.

She leaned forward more as she felt her own climax slowly building, gently being stroked.

That move exposed more of her core, her pink lips gripping him, and Lex couldn't look away for the life of him as his rod glistened with their juices.

She felt him stiffen like iron in her and against her. She knew he would come. *They* would come. She deepened her grind, her heart pumping wildly, anxiousness building because she knew she would ride the highs of her climax. "I felt it get harder," she told him.

"It's gon' come. Don't...stop. Nice and slow. Just like that. Just...like...that."

April smiled at the lack of control in his voice as he began to grind his hips up against her. They slipped right into one unified rhythm. One erotic slow grind. A sexual hustle.

Both began to tremble with that first wave of release but they kept the rhythm. Didn't break the grind. Nice and slow. Easy.

Lex felt his feet stiffen and warm just before the first of his seed shot into her. "Aaaghhhh," he cried out, biting the side of his tongue to keep from hollering like a woman.

April sat up straight, never breaking their rhythm as she raised her hand above her head like she was riding a bronco. A well-hung bronco.

"Damn, girl. Damn!" His hips jerked up off the bed.

She softly giggled with euphoria as she rode the wave of her own climax. Nice and slow. Easy. "Oh Lex," she sighed in pleasure letting her eyes drift close. "Oh, Lex, I'm coming. I'm coming all over you, baby."

"Come on. Come," he urged thickly. Loving the way she flung her head back so far until her hair swung to the top of her buttocks, Lex felt his rod hardening again.

He sat up straight and wrapped his arms around her to tightly grasp her full breasts with each hand as she worked the last of his release from him.

That pushed her over the edge, and April hollered out hoarsely as she felt herself free-falling. Weightless. Endless.

Moments later she collapsed back against him, glad that his arms held her tightly.

Chapter 3

Going to the Chapel

April entered her hotel room, careful not to awaken Clayton as she closed the door and moved into the room. He loved sleeping in on a Sunday morning, and she imagined that wouldn't change even in Vegas.

The room was suddenly flooded with light.

"That good that you spent the night or that bad that you left first thing in the morning?"

April looked at Clayton in his bed, bare-chested with the sheet up to his hips as he sat up. "Waiting up?" she asked dryly as she sat down on her bed and kicked off her shoes.

"More like getting up. It's seven in the morning."

"It was one of those nights," April lied. Last night had been nothing like any other night in her life. Ever.

"Tell me about him."

April reached behind herself to unzip her dress. "Who?"

"Stop playing games, April," Clayton said in a strong voice.

"I just don't feel like talking about it right now, but I will. I will." April rose and the dress fell to a black puddle around her feet. She was exhausted. Spent. Emotionally and physically.

"Cool."

She walked into the bathroom and started a shower. As the steam began to rise around her, April looked at her reflection in the mirror. She looked like the same old April, but she wasn't.

She thought of him. She whispered his full name, "Alexander Macmillan". A chill raced from her head to her polished toes.

What she shared with him had been beyond sex. April was no innocent by any means, but g with him had felt like all the good things n life combined into one sensation. She had lain awake and watched him as he slept. She had yearned to wake him to hear his voice. She had cuddled her face against his chest and inhaled his scent. She hated the thought of never seeing him again.

And all of that scared the devil out of her.

April allowed herself one last kiss to his lips before she left him and dressed in the quiet of the foyer. She ran. She had never felt such an intense connection with someone before, and that wasn't good for a one-night stand.

And wasn't that all it was? A one-night stand.

He would be back with his boys enjoying all the T & A across the Vegas strip while she tried her best to enjoy the rest of her vacation without craving him. So she ran to avoid any awkward, morning-after, stilted conversation and lies of phone calls to come.

April sighed as she looked at herself, at the thought of never seeing him again. One lone tear raced down her cheek just before the steam covered her reflection.

The banging on a door woke Lex with a jolt from his sleep. For a second he was lost to time or place as he looked left and then right. "What the—"

He flung back the covers and sat up on the side of the bed as he wiped the sleep from his eyes.

The banging continued.

"Damn," he swore, snatching the sheet off the rumpled bed to wrap around his waist as he rose and made his way to the suite's front door.

His body felt drained of all energy. It was a task to raise each foot to take the steps. He nearly stumbled over his shoe in the foyer as he snatched the door open. "What?" he roared.

Derrick and War strolled past Lex into the suite.

"What happened to you last night?" Derrick asked.

"Yeah, how are you gon' ditch my bachelor party?" War piped in.

Suddenly Lex remembered *just* what he did last night. He nearly tripped over the sheet as he dashed through the living room and dining room to reach the bedroom. Empty bed. His grasp on the sheet slackened as he walked into the two master baths. Both were empty.

Where is she?

Naked he made his way to the bed and picked up one of the many pillows. Her scent clung to it and he inhaled it deeply.

"Whoa, man. Put on some clothes," War said from behind him.

"That's way more of you than I needed to see. Trust me, dawg," Derrick added.

He looked and they both were standing in the bedroom with their backs turned to him. Lex moved to his bathroom and grabbed his robe to put on. "I'm straight," he said, tying it tightly around his waist as he walked back into the bedroom.

They both turned around.

"What the hell happened to you last night, dawg?"

Lex thought of her. April Dutton. His heart raced. He had never felt as alive, as self-assured, and as satisfied with life in general, as he did yesterday in her company and then last night in her arms.

It would've been better to wake up with her at his side than feel a bit used because she got the goods all night and then ran out. What they shared had been like nothing else he'd ever felt. Everything about their union had seemed right. Complete. Satisfying.

And now she was gone.

I guess I just had my first one-night stand.

That thought didn't sit well with him.

War and Derrick were looking at him, waiting for an answer.

"I just chilled out all night. I needed the rest."

War and Derrick exchanged a disbelieving look.

Lex ignored them. He wanted to go find April. She was somewhere in this hotel. Why did she leave?

"We're headed down to breakfast. A brother hungrier than a mother," Derrick said, rubbing his washboard abdomen.

Lex's stomach grumbled, protesting its emptiness. "I guess I am, too."

"Get dressed and let's roll. The rest of the fellas are already downstairs." War walked to the bedroom door.

"Actually y'all go ahead. I still have to wash and make a few phone calls."

War and Derrick exchanged another disbelieving look.

"What?" Lex asked in innocence.

"We'll be at the café," War said, before turning and striding out of the suite.

Derrick turned and walked out of the room, as well. He turned suddenly at the door. "You okay, dawg?" he asked, his eyes squinting as he looked at Lex.

Lex smiled broadly and held up his hands. "I'm straight," he insisted.

Derrick said nothing and just turned to walk out of the suite.

Lex dropped his robe and hurried through a quick shower before dressing in linen slacks and a fitted white T-shirt. He slid his wallet into his back pocket and grabbed his cell phone before striding out of the hotel suite.

He was going to find April.

"Are you going to mope in bed all day?" Clayton asked as he put on his leather-banded watch.

April nodded from where she lay in the center of her bed propped up on all of her pillows and the pillows from Clayton's bed as she flipped through the television channels.

Clayton slid his strong hands into the pockets of his black silk-lined pants. "I don't know whose penis you ran into last night but that's one I don't want to know."

April shifted her eyes to him and smiled. "It was good, too," she admitted with a wink.

Clayton sat down on the edge of her bed. "Then why aren't you still with it?"

She bit her bottom lip, trying to think of a way to verbalize her fear—the same fear that had her scrambling for the door—without sounding or feeling crazy. "It was *too* good."

Clayton laughed. "No such thing."

"The best I ever had," she stressed with a pointed look.

"That's saying a lot," Clayton countered dryly.

April pulled a pillow from behind her and swung it at his handsome square face. "Shut up. I'm being serious, Clayton."

"Turned you inside out, huh?"

"Yes, but it was more than that. I've had good sex—hell, great sex—but this was emotional and electrifying and all that mushy crap you read in romance books."

Clayton reached out and massaged her foot under the coverlet.

"Great sex, definitely. More positions than Kama Sutra, sure. A three-minute orgasm, yes..."

Clayton whistled. "*That's* impressive."

"But I have never felt so in tune, so alive, so connected to a man before."

"And that scared you."

"It scared the shit out of me, especially for

what was a Vegas fling for us both. It was way too deep. So I ran."

"How do you know he didn't feel that way?"

"Because I know."

"How?"

"I just know."

"How?"

April leveled her eyes with his. "Because I...just...know."

There was a knock at the outer door.

"That's probably Raoul," Clayton said, rising and leaving the room. "We're going to a show."

April pulled the cozy covers up closer to her chin and snuggled down deeper into the plush pillows as she resumed flipping through the channels. She paused at a scene of a man carrying a woman to bed as they kissed.

She shivered as she remembered being in Lex's arms. Arms that felt like they were meant to hold her...just her. Amazing how she felt relief and sadness at the thought of never seeing him again.

She heard Clayton walking back into the bedroom as she flipped onto her side, intent on enjoying a rerun of *Sanford and Son.* "You going? Have fun."

Some emotion lightly skimmed over her

body, and April looked up to instead find Lex lounging in the doorway. Her heart slammed against her chest like a car slamming on brakes.

He smiled down at her, and April felt her fears replaced with utter joy as she smiled in return.

"Hey you," Lex began, thinking she looked adorable in the middle of the plushly covered bed.

"Hey."

"What you watching?"

"Sanford and Son."

He nodded. "Good choice."

"Yup."

"That bed looks comfortable."

"It is."

"Can I join you?"

He couldn't believe the nerves knotting his stomach as he awaited her answer. He smiled when she held the edges of the cover up. He kicked off his shoes and climbed beneath the covers pulling her pajama-clad body close to his side.

And she felt good—damn good—in his arms.

"How did you find me?" she asked, her hand lightly caressing the hand he rested gently against her abdomen.

"I can be very resourceful," he said. No need to tell her I knocked on every door on this floor. "So why did you run out on me?"

"I hate messy goodbyes," she said, tilting her head away from him a bit.

Lex pressed her down onto her back and then leaned down to stare into her face. "Who said anything about goodbye?"

She lightly licked her lips as her eyes fell to his mouth. "Huh?"

Lex smiled before lowering his head to capture her lips with his own. "Just as good as I remembered," he whispered into her mouth.

"Aren't you going back to New York today?" she asked, her eyes hesitant.

"Suddenly I feel like a few days vacationing in Vegas with a beautiful, sexy and funny lady is more to my liking. You game?"

Her hand came up to wrap around his neck as she pulled him down and deepened the kiss with a soft purr that made his heart race.

"Yo, man, where's Lex?" War asked, as the men all awaited the minibus scheduled to take them to the airport for their afternoon flights back to their respective cities.

"Good damn question," Derrick said, whipping out his BlackBerry. "I'll try his phone again because a brotha 'bout to get left."

He eyed a voluptuous woman walking by as Lex's phone rang.

"Yeah."

"Lex? What, you sleeping?" Derrick asked in astonishment, drawing the eyes of War and the rest of their friends.

"What time is it?"

"It's five seconds from you missing your ride to the damn plane." Derrick squinted through his shades as the bus pulled to a stop at the curb.

"Damn. I meant to call y'all sooner. I'm staying in Vegas for the rest of the week."

Derrick's eyes widened in surprise as he handed his leather duffel to the driver and then climbed onto the minibus that looked more like an intimate corner of a nightclub. "Whoever she is she must have a motor in that thing," Derrick joked.

"She? She who?" War asked.

Derrick tilted the mouthpiece away. "Lex is staying in Vegas for a week."

War made a face. "Lex?" he asked in disbelief.

"Yeah, I know, right."

"Tell him he better not miss my wedding," War warned.

"Tell War I heard him. Call me when you land."

"No problem. Oh, and Lex, strap it up all the time, every time."

"No doubt."

Derrick closed his cell phone. "Lex that sly little dog."

"Of all the fellas to get sprung in Vegas. Lex? Mr. Sensible? Mr. Responsibility?" War asked, crossing his arms over his chest as he leaned back against the leather seating.

Derrick smiled, shaking his head. "I'll be damned."

One Week Later

April's eyelids were heavy with relaxation as she lay atop a padded massage table on her stomach. She gazed over at Lex on a similar massage table beside her in the Watsu Room of the Bellagio Spa. "This should be illegal," she murmured, her voice drowsy as the masseuse kneaded her feet with skill.

Lex grunted in response as his own masseuse worked her magic on his scalp.

As a surprise—one of many over the past three days—Lex scheduled a three-hour-long couple's spa package. During a tandem soak in a heated pool, a therapist had taught them to float each other in the water. Every bit of the hour-long experience had been a heightening of their tantric senses around each other. Of course, it wasn't meant to feel so sexual, but everything between April and Lex felt that way and the soak was no exception.

After a small break for a private lunch Lex had arranged for them, the couple began a relaxing hour-long hand, foot and scalp massage that was sinfully good. Last they were scheduled for a twenty-five-minute body polishing to refresh the skin.

April could hardly believe the time she spent with Lex in Vegas. They were inseparable while they took in the sights, caught some shows, gambled or just lounged and enjoyed the beauty of the Bellagio. They went to bed together every night in his penthouse suite, and April thought she'd never slept so peacefully as she did in his arms.

For three days they were lost in each other. She barely took time to call her sister or even check in with Clayton—who was lost in his own romance with Raoul—because she reveled in the time she was spending with Lex.

But that was coming to an end.

That same fear she felt their first night together nearly choked her as she imagined them actually saying goodbye and going their separate ways.

"Wow, you became really tense suddenly," Helga the masseuse said with a hint of laughter in her voice.

April felt Lex's eyes on her as she forced herself to relax. She smiled at him and tried her best to keep the sadness from her eyes.

Lex reached out his hand to her, and April slid her hand into his. When he squeezed her hand, comforting and reassuring, she felt as if he was letting her know that he knew exactly how she was feeling.

And that made her feel even closer to him.

The fountains of Bellagio were a mix of well-orchestrated water, lights and music. Lex first saw the display in the *Ocean's Twelve* movie, and he had been intrigued by it then, but to stand before it was majestic. The entire crowd of people standing behind the waist-high wrought-iron fence were quiet—maybe a bit awestruck.

Lex looked down at April and saw the show reflected in her eyes as she smiled softly in pleasure. Damn, I'm going to miss her, he thought as he lightly rested his hand on the small of her back.

"I could stand here and watch this forever," April said, as she glanced up at him.

"I could watch you forever." Lex laughed softly and smiled. "That sounds corny."

"But very sweet," she replied, reaching up to lightly stoke his smooth cheek.

Lex leaned his head down a bit to taste her lips.

"I wish I knew what song's playing now," she said, turning her attention back to the fountains.

"It's '*Con Te Partiro.*'"

"You speak Spanish?" she asked in surprise.

"Enough to get by."

"What is the song about?"

"*Con te partiro* means 'time to say goodbye.'" He watched her profile intently as she watched the fountains and the lights and listened to the beauty of the duet. He ached to see the tears filling her eyes.

This was their last night together, and the thought of not sleeping with her in his arms and waking up with her still there bothered him.

"Marry me," he said suddenly.

April stiffened and turned slowly to look up at him. "What? Huh? Who? Huh?"

Lex dropped to one knee and gathered April's hands in both of his own. "April, I don't want this week to end. I never expected to find someone as exciting and beautiful and vibrant as you. I feel like we shouldn't let this end. Marry me? Marry me right now."

A crowd gathered around them and gasped just as the fountains shot straight up to the sky like geysers and the music reached a crescendo. It was an awe-inspiring, albeit clichéd romantic moment.

"Yes," she gasped. "Yes."

Lex rose and gathered April to him for a deep kiss that she returned with vigor and passion.

The next morning April awakened on her stomach and took a deep and leisurely stretch. She lifted her head from the pillow and looked over to find Lex's side of the bed empty.

Lex was her husband.

April rolled over onto her back and kicked her feet in the air in a childlike fashion. Today was the first day of the rest of their lives.

Last night they had driven straight to the Clark County Marriage Bureau for their marriage license and then headed to The Little White Chapel for their ceremony. A ceremony that was surprisingly romantic, considering.

"Lex," she called out, rolling out of bed to pull on his discarded shirt before she left the bedroom to seek out her husband.

She found him in the living room sitting before the ornate coffee table. "Good morning, hubby o' mine, how 'bout we order up some breakfast?"

Lex lifted his head, and the look on his face made April's stomach drop. She saw the regret before he even spoke the words. "We made a mistake, April."

"What do you mean?" she asked, crossing her arms over her ample chest.

"I got up this morning to make arrangements for us to leave Vegas today, and I realized we didn't think this through. Are you moving to New York with me? Are you giving up your job? What does your family think about all this, and God knows what mine will think."

She watched him as he rose and began pacing. "I don't care what my family thinks. I'm grown."

"Easy for you to say. My situation is certainly different."

"What does that mean?"

"Here in Vegas our differences back in the real world didn't matter—"

"What differences?" she asked, her voice soft and easy. But that was deceptive.

"I have business, social and family obligations you wouldn't understand or even be able to comprehend. Responsibilities. Expectations. This marriage is not acceptable."

"'Comprehend?'" April laughed bitterly. "Don't you really mean *I'm* not acceptable?"

Lex turned and looked straight at her. "That's not what I said. Don't twist my words."

"No, not your words but your thoughts. Same difference." April turned and strode into the bedroom to begin gathering her clothes. She felt anger rising as she gathered the clothes into a ball and shoved them under her arm. She nearly collided with Lex as he strode into the room.

"April, listen, we—"

"*You*...asked...me, Lex," she told him, jabbing his chest with her finger. "You asked me."

His eyes flashed with some emotion as his face registered the truth of her words.

"You already were getting the damn milk for free all week long, you didn't have to buy the cow for a night."

He reached out to lightly grasp her upper arms. "I don't regret this week I spent with you."

April tilted her head to the side as she looked up at him with pained eyes. "But you regret marrying me?" she asked in a soft, husky voice.

His eyes shifted from hers, and she stepped back from his grasp.

"April, I didn't quite think of the repercussions of this—"

"So you want a divorce?" she asked, even as the anger dissolved into hurt.

"Actually my lawyer said—"

Ouch. "So you've already talked to your attorney?" she asked in disbelief.

"Yes, yes I did," Lex admitted as he looked down at her.

April turned and walked out of the living room to the foyer. She removed his shirt, allowing herself one final sniff of his all-too-familiar scent, before she began to dress quickly.

"April."

She paused for a second, and she felt hope rise in her chest as she envisioned him pulling her into his arms and telling her they would fight for the connection they made this week, they would fight for their marriage, they would fight for each other…come what may.

"The annulment papers will be here in an hour. Will you be in your room?"

April closed her eyes and fought the wave of pain. She finished dressing and nodded, not allowing herself to turn and look at him as she walked out of the penthouse suite without another word.

Chapter 4

Have You Seen Her?
New York, New York

"Are you okay, son? You seem to have a lot on your mind."

Lex had been staring off down the green of the golf course, but he turned his head to look over at his father, Harris "Big Mac" Macmillan. "Nothing I can't handle," he answered.

"Anything to do with your extended time in Vegas?" Big Mac asked with a sidelong glance at his son.

Lex didn't even comment. As soon as they discovered he was back in New York, his parents headed straight to his apartment to make clear their disapproving feelings about him leaving the helm of the company for a week to "play" in Vegas. He wasn't touching that subject again with a ten-foot pole.

"If there's anything I can do to help, son, let me know."

Lex stepped up to take his position with his tee and golf ball. Nothing major, Dad, I just need to find my wife and get her to sign annulment papers. That's all. Nothing big.

Lex took his position and swung his golf club effortlessly, sending the ball far off into the distance. He watched it with eaglelike attention as it landed just a couple of feet from the eighth hole.

"Good shot, son."

Lex smiled, though his thoughts were elsewhere.

When he awakened yesterday morning to April as his wife, he had kissed her softly and made his way to the living room to make their travel arrangements without disturbing her. But in the light of day, reality had set in for him big-time.

They were from two different states, but

even more so, two different worlds. April's free-spirited and wild nature had been fun and intoxicating in Vegas but back in New York how could she possibly fit into his life? He was from a wealthy family, and there was an expectation for him to marry a certain "type" of woman. Someone with as much money, class, breeding and sophistication as he.

He had always been brought up to believe there were two types of women: the ones you screw and the ones you marry. April didn't fall into the latter, but he had enjoyed her company. Truthfully he had needed the days in Vegas with her just as he needed air.

Lex released a heavy breath. His actions were usually so methodical and so well thought out. The one time he decided to follow his desires and be impulsive, he wound up marrying a woman he'd only known for a week in Vegas!

He could just imagine his parents' reaction if they knew that fact, and that he hadn't even signed a prenuptial. Double whammy.

I have got to get those annulment papers signed.

Easier said than done when he couldn't get in contact with his runaway bride.

When he'd gone to April's room it was to find that she and Clayton were gone. He'd been calling her cell phone and leaving voicemail messages since yesterday. He felt foolish to admit he couldn't remember the home address she put on the application for their marriage license. He was already working on getting a copy of that.

She was in Richmond, Virginia. That he knew. The rest he would know soon and he was headed to Richmond to get her signature on the dotted line.

His heart raced at the thought of seeing her again.

He was man enough to admit he missed her.

"Warrick all ready for the wedding Saturday?" Big Mac asked as they climbed into the golf buggy and continued across the green to the next hole.

"Yeah, that's what he says." Lex climbed from the cart and selected a golf club.

"Marriage isn't to be taken lightly. It's a serious commitment."

"True," Lex chimed in, feeling like a hypocrite.

"You know what my daddy always told me—"

"Never start something you can't finish."

Big Mac took his swing, and the sound of the club hitting the golf ball echoed. "Damn right."

Richmond, Virginia

April looked up from where she sat in the middle of her bed as her bedroom door opened slowly and Gabby peeked her head inside.

"Ready for some company?" Gabby asked, using her shoulder to open the door as she walked in holding the baby in her arms.

"Only if you are done with your tirade on how foolish, irresponsible and childish I am when I *want* to be."

"I promise. And I brought the peacemaker." She stepped inside the bedroom and showed April her nephew.

April sat up and smiled. "I always have time for him," she said, holding out her arms and then cuddling him close to her chest.

"You ready to talk about it?"

"About what? Going to Vegas and making a fool out of myself behind some man?" April asked. "Yes, sure, let's talk about stupid Ape and some more of her man drama."

Gabrielle sat on the bed and reached out to lightly rub her sister's leg. "You've been crying," she observed.

"My eyes swollen?"

Gabby nodded. “Looks like bees stung your eyelids.”

They laughed a little.

April looked down at her nephew’s angelic face. “I really thought I had found my Prince Charming. I let good—no great—sex and a little romantic attention mess my head up.”

“What did Clayton say about all this?”

April looked up. “He doesn’t know.”

“What?”

“No one knows but you.”

“And Maxwell.” Gabrielle added.

April gave her sister a look. She had a play-play, love/hate relationship with her brother-in-law. They argued and debated anything and everything and the last thing April wanted to do was give him material to tease her about. A Britney Spears–type Vegas wedding was just the thing for him to run into the ground.

“Don’t make me have to clock that husband of yours,” April warned, only half teasing.

Gabrielle just laughed.

“I just wanted to fly home drama free, and get away from Vegas as fast as I could tuck my ass between my legs, little sister.”

“What happened?” Gabby asked with a puzzled expression.

April gave her sister the digest version of her relationship with Alexander "Lex" Macmillan. As she spoke the words and relived the memories, she relished the emotions attached to every moment. Surprise. Excitement. Pleasure. Happiness.

Sadness. Their last moments together in his suite were nothing but sad memories for her.

"So you wanted to stay married?"

April shrugged. "I didn't want him to make me feel like I wasn't good enough for him and his big-time family back in New York," April said, anger flashing in her eyes.

"His loss."

April smiled at her sister and then lifted the baby to snuggle her face into his neck and inhale deeply of his sweet innocence.

April's "Disco Inferno" ring tone sounded from her bedside table.

The sisters locked eyes.

April reached over with her free hand and picked up the cell phone. She felt an odd mix of relief and disappointment to see his phone number on the caller ID. "There's the old ball and chain now," April quipped, focusing her attention on the baby who was now awake and cooing.

"You have to talk to him eventually, Ape."

"True."

"You need to get this thing annulled."

"Right again, sis."

The phone stopped ringing.

"When are you going to call him and get this thing straightened out?" Gabby asked.

"I've decided to go to New York in the morning."

"You are?" Gabby asked. "Does he know you're coming?"

"He'll know I'm in the Big Apple when I get ready because trust me, little sister, I *got* his number."

Lex checked his watch as he climbed out of the taxi carrying his garment bag from Mohan Custom Tailors. He quickly paid the driver from his monogrammed money clip as the heavy traffic of New York continued past him.

It was a little after twelve. After his early-morning golf game with his father, he'd gone straight to the tailor to pick up his tuxedo for the wedding in two days. Traffic caused him to be tardy for his lunch date with War, Elizabeth and their mutual friend Tiffany Hightower.

Truthfully, if he hadn't decided to extend his time away from the office until Monday, he would be so deep in meetings that they wouldn't have seen him at all.

As he walked into Tavern on the Green, Lex reached for his cell phone and tried her number for what had to be the millionth time since she walked out of his hotel suite in Vegas on Wednesday.

"This is Ape. Talk to me."

He didn't bother leaving a voice mail. He tried that already to no avail.

"Good afternoon, Mr. Macmillan. May I take your garment bag for you while you're dining?"

Lex nodded as he handed the bag to the portly maître d'. "Thank you, Walter."

"Mr. Kinsey and the rest of your party are awaiting you."

Lex slid his cell phone back into the inner pocket of his custom-made lightweight silk suit as he followed the man to their table. "Hello everyone."

"We thought you were going to stand us up again, Alexander." Tiffany presented her slender hand to him, the epitome of style, grace, charm and manners.

He smiled warmly at her as he kissed the smooth back of her hand. "And miss lunch with two beautiful ladies?" he asked.

She smiled.

The waiter promptly appeared at Lex's elbow. Once he placed his order for stuffed salmon and wild rice he looked to his best friend and his fiancée. "Are the lovebirds ready for Saturday? It's just about forty-eight hours and counting."

Elizabeth slid her hand around War's brawny arm and squeezed it tightly. "I can hardly wait to be Mrs. Warrick Kinsey," she sighed.

Lex looked on as War leaned his head down lightly to capture her perfectly pursed lips with his own. He felt Tiffany's eyes on him, but Lex directed his gaze to some random spot across the restaurant.

Lex was quite aware that his socialite childhood friend would be just as pleased to be Mrs. Alexander Macmillan. Maybe even more than his mother wished for the couple. On paper they were the perfect match. Just the type of match his mother—a socialite in her own right—would want him to make.

Tiffany's parents were wealthy and politically influential business owners whose familial wealth could be dated back to inheritances received since post-slavery days. Just like the families of everyone at the table. They were a part of the "black elite" who didn't have the same respect for those first-generation wealthy blacks. Social-class discrimination at its worst.

And Tiffany had been groomed to be the perfect wife. She had an excellent Spellman education, held leadership in her sorority, was a card-carrying member of the NAACP and the Urban League. Never missed church. Volunteered in various organizations.

Beautiful. Genteel. A lady in every sense of the word even down to the pearls.

But as far as Lex was concerned, Tiffany was no more than a childhood best friend. Never had he thought of her in any other way, although he knew she wanted otherwise.

Lex stopped their waiter. "May we have a bottle of Krug's Clos du Mesnil champagne, please?"

"Right away, sir."

"Good choice, Lex," War added.

"Now, Lex, you know Lizzie and I do not drink," Tiffany said. "Could you imagine what our parents would say?"

Elizabeth raised both her brows before the ladies broke out with laughter.

"Well, my parents don't care if I drink, so bring it on," War said.

Lex heard a bit of an edge to his friend's voice, and his eyes rested on him lightly in question before he shifted them away. The waiter arrived and made a ceremony of opening the bottle and presenting it to Lex before filling the four crystal flutes he carried.

Lex raised his flute in the center of the table. "A toast for two of the best people I know."

"Tiff, we have got to get in on this," Elizabeth said, leaning forward to pick up her own flute.

Tiffany did the same. "Just a sip."

War took Elizabeth's free hand into his own.

And at that moment, as he watched War and Elizabeth, Lex thought of his own nuptials just two days ago. It was amazing to him how much he missed her. Sad how their marriage had brought an end to their dealings instead of drawing them together. In truth, he longed for April until his chest hurt and the light of his soul dimmed a bit.

But there was no time for "if only."

He released a small, composing breath. "Here's to happy endings," he finished softly.

"Here, here."

They all touched their flutes with multiple dings.

April hadn't smoked a cigarette since her twenties. Vanity had led to her stop when her lips began to darken in color, but a range of emotions about Lex had her back at it again.

She inhaled deeply of the Newport as she sat on the small stoop outside the guest house—currently her house—of Maxwell and Gabby's Richmond estate. The sun was gone and the night sky was lit up with stars. The moon was so full and magnificent that she felt she could just reach her hand up and touch it.

I have business, social and family obligations. Responsibilities. Expectations. This is not acceptable.

April smirked a little as she released a stream of silver smoke.

The annulment papers will be here in an hour.

The same dart of pain and disbelief that struck her chest when he first said the words, stung again.

April rose and made her way up the path to the main house, finishing the cigarette. She smelled something delicious that Addie was cooking and was surprised when her stomach grumbled, protesting its emptiness. She hadn't eaten a decent meal since she left Vegas yesterday. Her emotions had her full.

April entered the house via the kitchen entrance and found Addie stirring at a pot. The older woman looked up as April closed the window-paned door behind her.

"Hey, Ape. You just in time for some smothered pork chops and mash potatoes. I'm trying like the devil to get some meat on your sister's bones."

April smiled. Addie had that effect on everyone. She was feisty, outspoken and could be funnier than Cedric the Entertainer and Steve Harvey combined, when she wanted to. And everyone loved her to death, especially Maxwell. So much so that he'd hired her on as the housekeeper/cook ages ago. But she'd never put broom to floor, and when she got up in age he convinced her to move onto the estate. She no longer "worked" for him, but he faithfully paid her every week just like always. Now she cooked her delicious southern treats because she wanted to. There wasn't a blood link, but Addie was family.

"Is Clayton coming over for dinner?" Addie asked.

"I doubt it." April walked over to Addie and hugged her round body to her side. "Where's that brother-in-law of mine?"

"Where else? You know he's getting ready for a new exhibit."

April smiled. "He in a good mood?"

Addie bumped her hip against April's. "Your sister had me keep an eye on the baby for 'bout an hour while she carried herself up to that studio with nothing on but a smile. Like I didn't see her. I'm old not blind. Holla back."

April laughed. Addie had a penchant for dropping hip-hop lingo at the oddest moments. "Well, I'm going up to catch him while he's still feeling the afterglow."

"Tell him and Gabby dinner's ready," Addie called behind her.

April jogged up the stairs to the top level of the house to Maxwell's studio. She knocked briefly, her stomach a little nervous as she awaited his approval to enter.

"Come in."

April walked in and found Maxwell in his usual paint-stained jeans and T-shirt standing before an easel, his palette in one hand and a paintbrush in the other. "Hey, bossman. Addie said dinner's ready."

"What's the deal, Mrs. Macmillan?" he asked with a sly smile as he turned back to his easel.

"Real funny, you Picasso wannabe," she returned.

Maxwell flung his head back and laughed. "A Picasso wannabe that pays your salary, though. Ha."

April just smiled as she walked up to him. "Is that for the Guggenheim?"

He nodded, biting the tip of the paint brush as he studied his work. "Can I help you with something?"

"A thousand dollars." There I said it.

Maxwell turned and looked down at her. "Would I be wrong to ask what for?"

"Maybe. Maybe not."

"And would I be wrong to ask what a woman who doesn't pay rent or buy food or have a car does with her salary?"

April locked eyes with him. "You would be dead wrong."

He nodded slowly, reflectively. "Now I *will* ask—when will I get my money back?"

April actually smiled. "Cut my salary by two hundred a week for five weeks. Deal?"

"Deal."

April watched as Maxwell pulled out his wallet and counted ten crisp one-hundred-dollar bills. She accepted it when he handed it over to her. "You dead wrong to walk around with all that money in your wallet."

"I don't usually."

"Thanks, Maxwell." April turned and walked to the door.

"Hey, Ape."

April turned at the door.

"You okay?"

"I will be," she promised, leaving the studio and closing the door behind her.

April was determined to be okay. She refused to let a man get the best of her. She was hurt and disappointed, but mainly she was angry and getting angrier by the second, the minute and the increasing hours.

How dare he make her feel like she wasn't good enough for high society? That she couldn't *comprehend* his life? That she was not an *acceptable* component of his life.

Alexander Macmillan didn't know who he was playing with.

The longer she had sat and thought, the

more she had plotted and planned. It was time to teach Mr. Alexander Macmillan a lesson. And, to ensure that no one could talk her out of it, April had made the decision not to tell a living soul just what she had planned for her husband.

Chapter 5

Guess Who's Coming to Dinner
New York, New York

Lex had decided to go into the office today. Why not? It kept his mind off his confusing feelings of wanting desperately to find April and get the wedding annulled but also desiring her smile and her body and her presence in general.

He craved her, but he knew he had to get over her. They were from two different worlds, and his world, for all of its facade of properness and etiquette, would eat a woman like April alive.

"Good morning, Mr. Macmillan."

Lex nodded in greeting to the doorman, Wilson, as he walked out of the Madison Avenue building where the Macmillan, Inc. offices were located. With the *New York Times* and the *Wall Street Journal* folded under his arm, Lex strode forward as the doorman quickened his steps to then open the door to the limousine awaiting Lex at the curb. "Thank you."

"Good evening, sir." Wilson shut the limo door.

"Abyssinia Baptist Church, Reginald," Lex instructed his driver of the past four years.

He read the papers during the twenty-minute congested drive to the church for the rehearsal of War and Elizabeth's wedding the next day. He was enjoying a feature article on the advertising industry—one in which he was quoted concerning current trends—when his phone rang.

He pulled his silver SmartPhone from his inner breast pocket. "Alexander Macmillan."

"Hello, hubbie."

His heart literally slammed against his chest

at the sound of April's voice. He envisioned her. Remembered her scent. Her taste. Her sex. Her smile. He took a breath—a deep one. "How are you, April?"

"I'm good, but then, you already know that, don't you?"

He smiled and dropped his head. "I'm glad you returned my calls...finally."

"Umph. Had you sweating?"

"Not really."

"Don't be flip, dear, it doesn't become you."

"Is this a game to you, April?" he asked, his eyes shifting to look out at the urban landscape.

"A game is fun, dear. Waking up to find out your husband has already called his lawyer for annulment papers before you could take a morning whizz ain't fun at all. Trust."

Lex pressed the phone to his ear as if to be closer to her.

"You're quiet. What are you thinking of?" she asked huskily.

"You," he answered with honesty. "Vegas. Us."

"There is no us."

"I think Clark County and The Little White Chapel in Vegas would say otherwise."

"That's just a piece of paper."

"An important piece of paper," he stressed,

choosing his words carefully because he wasn't quite sure where April's head was.

"And you have a more important piece of paper that you would like me to sign, don't you?" She laughed a little.

Lex frowned. "We rushed into marriage and you know that as well as I do, but I never said it had to be over between us for good."

"If I'm not good enough to marry then I sure ain't good enough to screw."

The limo pulled to a stop before the church. "So you never want to see me again, April?" he asked.

"Two days ago I thought I would see you and hold you and sex you every day of my life for the rest of my life," she countered.

Lex froze. "It's just not that simple."

The line went quiet.

Lex left his briefcase and his newspapers on the seat as he got out of the limousine. The sky was just beginning to darken with evening. "You still there?"

"Yup."

"I'm sorry. I never wanted to hurt you."

"Humph."

"April?" Lex held the phone to his face and tilted his square and strong chin to the sky. "I can fly out to you in Richmond and bring the papers Sunday."

"Or you can overnight them to me and that way we don't have to see each other again. That sounds like a better plan to me."

How odd that her suggestion they never see each other again hurt his feelings. Damn, was he crazy? What did he want—the cake and the ice cream?

Yes, he wanted the marriage ended but he wanted to bury himself deep within her walls until the were both breathless and weak. Sweaty and sated. Excited and tired. All at once.

"Hey, Lex, whassup man?"

Lex looked up and shook hands briefly with Derrick, who was on *his* phone. "Whaddup."

"Everyone inside?" Derrick asked.

"I guess. I'm running late and I just got here."

"Are you going to the rehearsal dinner?" Derrick asked.

Lex nodded, holding the phone away from his mouth a bit. "Definitely. I skipped lunch *and* it's at Justin's."

"That's what I'm talking about." Derrick jogged up the stairs and into the church.

"Yeah. Sorry 'bout that, April?" Lex frowned at the dead line. "April?"

"Damn," he swore, quickly dialing her cell phone number again. It rang three times and went to voice mail. "April, call me back as soon as you get this."

"Lex? Lex?"

He looked up to find Tiffany waving him in from the church door.

"Everyone's waiting on you," she said.

He jogged up the stairs to reach her.

"Looking handsome as always," she said, lightly touching her hand to his lapel as he leaned down to kiss her cheek. "And smelling good, too."

Lex smiled with charm and he pressed a hand to the small of her back as they walked into the church. "Ah, you're making me blush," he said, trying to keep the exchange light and friendly.

Tiffany pinched him playfully. "Oh, Lex, I just love you."

"Love you too, kid," he said, patting her cheek in a purely brotherly fashion.

April checked her makeup and her hair for the umpteenth time as she breathed deeply and fought off her nerves. There was no turning back now. She refused to turn back. She refused to believe he didn't deserve it.

Right?

April bit her thumbnail and then twisted her pinky ring. She took a deep sip of her cosmopolitan and then let her eyes dart around the restaurant. "What am I doing?" she mumbled frantically into her drink.

"May I join you?"

April looked up and found a tall, handsome brother with that sexy, dark, deep and delicious skin that made you wonder if he truly tasted like chocolate. In another place and at another time, April would have jumped on him...literally, but her plate was full for the evening.

"Actually I am waiting on someone but thank you."

"Lucky man," he said.

"No, not really. Trust me." April released a high hysterical laugh that made the man look down at her oddly as he walked away.

Come on, Ape. Get yourself together, girl.

There was activity at the door and her eyes darted to it just as a crowd of people walked in. Her gaze lit on her target as they were ushered toward a private area in the rear. *Showtime.*

April rose and smoothed her scarlet-red strapless tea-length dress over her hips as she moved through the restaurant. With each step she built her courage.

She paused, and at that moment Lex looked up and saw her. Her eyes registered the emotions that flittered across his face. Surprise. Confusion. Disbelief. Pleasure. And then desire. Lots of *desire.*

Her heart raced as their eyes locked and that familiar chemistry between them seemed to close the distance as it swelled in the area between them.

April stiffened her back. For a moment—a very brief moment—she felt what she was about to do was dead wrong. She plastered a big smile on her face and walked up to him with her arms open wide. "Oh, Lex, I have missed you so much," she said—just loud enough to be heard but not loud enough to look crazy—as she wrapped her arms around his strong neck and pressed her body and her lips to his.

When she felt his body loosen, his hands rise to sit on her hips and his lips heat, April almost forgot everything but the feel of him.

"Alexander? Who is this woman?"

April stepped back from him and then looked around him to the nearly fifteen pair of eyes gazing at them. She then stepped passed him with a huge Kool-Aid grin. He reached out slightly for her wrist, but she brushed him away without missing a beat. "Oh, hello. I'm sorry I didn't speak. I was so happy to see my Lex that I got caught up in the moment and lost my manners."

She felt him walk up behind her. She turned and saw that he was angry. She met his eyes with a challenge.

April reached up and stroked his cheek. "Don't you know what's done in the darkness always come to the light?"

"Don't do this, April," he said in a low and threatening tone.

"Now that I'm finally here, sweetie, let's make our announcement," she said, looking him dead in the eyes.

His eyes chilled.

April turned and faced the crowd. "I'm April. April Macmillan, Lex's wife, and I am so happy to meet each...and....every one of you."

"What!"

"Who is this woman?"

"Alexander, explain this immediately."

"What the hell?"

"Damn."

"I think the shit 'bout to hit the fan."

"Son, have you lost your mind?"

"She's fine, though."

Every comment, whispered and loudly spoken, echoed to Lex. He looked down at his mother—short, regal, loving and concerned—standing to the left of him. His wife stood to his right, looking beautiful, confident and far too satisfied with the melee unfolding around them.

Lex was a businessman, and his natural instinct was to go into immediate damage control. *Never let 'em see you sweat.* He slid his hand around April's waist, massaging her side as he smiled down at his mother as if the entire situation was natural.

"Mother. Father. Everyone, please excuse us for a moment," he said calmly as if he was in control. He felt anything but…yet.

"Alexander?" his mother called out, rising from her seat.

"We'll be right back," he said over his shoulder as he led April through the restaurant.

"There are plenty of witnesses," April said, giving him a sidelong glance. "So whatever you're wanting to do, remember that."

"I wanted to kiss you when I first saw you…before you pulled this stunt."

"And now?"

"Now I want to put you over my knee and spank you."

"Ooh, I like it when you talk dirty to me."

Lex led her out the door. "This isn't a game, April," he said in a hard voice.

She looked up at him. "You're right, it's not."

Lex slid his hands into his pockets as he looked down at her. "Do you know how much confusion in my life this will cause, April? Do you even care?"

"Not really."

Lex felt fury at her flippant attitude. "I wish I'd never carried my ass to Vegas in the first damn place."

"That makes two of us."

He saw the flash of pain in her eyes and felt guilty. "Look, April, we—"

"Alexander?"

He looked up to find his parents walking up to them.

"Are these my in-laws?" April asked, moving forward to meet them.

"Shit."

"Mr. and Mrs. Macmillan, it's so nice to meet

you both," she said, hugging them both close to her in an exaggerated fashion meant to annoy them.

"It's nice to meet you, as well. It would have been better to meet you before you married my son, dear," Mrs. Macmillan said, stepping back from April's embrace to move past her to Lex. "And you two *are* married?"

What to say? I'm the head of a major business and I married a woman after a week-long fling in Vegas?

"No—"

April left Big Mac's side to come stand by Lex's side. "No? Did you say...*no?*" she asked. "Did we not get married, Lex?"

Lex pinched the bridge of his nose, thinking that running a company was easier than dealing with this situation.

"Son?" his father asked in that big booming voice of his as he extracted a cigar from the platinum case in his breast pocket.

"Yes. Yes. April are I are married."

He felt April wrap her arm around his waist and hug him close. His father frowned deeply. He saw his mother falter back but only momentarily. She was always the epitome of composure, and not even finding out your only son—your only child—was married would crack the facade of propriety. Inside he knew she was seething.

"Lex? Everything okay?"

They all looked at War and Elizabeth walking up the sidewalk to them.

Candice Macmillan plastered a grin that was almost like the Joker's before she turned to the engaged couple. "Everything is fine, dear. We were just coming back in to finish celebrating with you. Come on, children."

Lex watched as April left his side to wrap her arm around Big Mac's. "I can see where Lex got his good looks, Mr. Macmillan."

"Big Mac. Everyone calls me Big Mac."

Just like that she had charmed his father. Everyone didn't call him that. Only family and friends.

He watched his mother stop, turn and shoot his father a look that would have sent a lesser man to his knees or the nearest jeweler.

April had bombarded herself into his life and proclaimed her spot as his wife. Now, what the hell was he going to do about it? She wasn't crazy or deranged. She wasn't a stalker. She was a woman scorned and wanting some payback. That was hell to deal with.

* * *

Everyone milled around outside the restaurant as they awaited the valets retrieving their numerous vehicles.

Tiffany was tired of smiling and laughing when she was mad enough and jealous enough to literally spit. Lex was married?

Why didn't he tell anyone?

Who was this woman?

Where did he meet her?

When did they marry?

Where did this leave her, when *she* had every intention of being Mrs. Alexander Macmillan?

"Everything is reversible, dear."

Tiffany turned to find Candice Macmillan standing behind her. She smiled at the woman she admired as a friend and a mentor. She bent to hug her petite frame. "What do you mean, Mrs. Macmillan?"

Candice reached out and stroked Tiffany's hand. "You're my choice for Alexander's wife, but you know that."

Tiffany nodded as she turned and looked at Lex and April talking to War and Elizabeth. "Too late for that now," she said with a trace of bitterness.

"Never too late. I always get what I want, my dear. Just watch and see."

Mrs. Macmillan strolled away to climb into the passenger seat of the silver Lexus with her husband.

"I hope so," she whispered, as the valet pulled up in her pale-gold BMW.

Tiffany remembered her training and walked over to the foursome. "Okay, Lizzie, time to tell War goodbye until tomorrow. We're off to my apartment to enjoy your last night being single," she said, surprised at how normal she sounded. "Next time you see him will be at the altar."

Elizabeth wrapped her arms around his waist and kissed him. "At the altar. That sounds good."

Tiffany turned to Lex. "See you tomorrow," she said reaching up to kiss his cheek.

She suddenly felt an arm shoot in between them.

"Yes, *we'll* see you tomorrow," April said.

"Yes…right. Alexander, we'll talk."

Tiffany walked away to climb behind the wheel of her vehicle. As soon as Elizabeth climbed into the passenger seat and closed the door, she sped off.

"I cannot believe Alexander," Candice said, smoothing the last of her moisturizer on her face before turning to join her husband in bed. "After the life we have given him, this is how he repays us by marrying that...that..."

Big Mac looked up from the book he was reading, *The Covenant with Black America*, to peer at his wife over the rim of his reading glasses. "That what? You don't even know that young lady."

Candice looked indignant. "That's my point exactly."

"You're not married to her."

"No, but my son is." She lay back amongst the pillows and pulled her mask down over her eyes. "Who are her parents? What is her career? What college did she go to? These—and many more—are important questions. Questions I *will* get answered tomorrow."

Chapter 6

Feel the Fire

"What do you want me from, April?"

"I don't want anything from you."

"Why are you here?"

"Maybe I wanted to see my husband. We're still in our honeymoon phase, remember?"

Lex strode across his study and lightly grasped April's shoulder to turn her to him. "This is a game to you," he stated, his eyes skimming her face.

April hated the awareness she had for him. Her entire body tingled and her skin felt scorched where his hands pressed into her soft flesh with familiarity. She felt as though an electrical current raced through their bodies.

She looked up at him and she saw the anger in his eyes flash to desire. She had wanted to make him suffer but at that moment she wanted nothing more than to be kissed by him.

"Damn, April, damn," he whispered even as his head lowered to hers. "I've missed you."

She gasped at the first feel of his lips, and her hands rose to stoke his body in his suit. Hard buttocks. Strong back. Broad shoulders. The softness of his hair against her fingertips as she caressed the back of his head as his tongue heatedly captured her own with a proprietary feel.

His hands lowered to grasp her buttocks before he shakily raised her dress up to her waist.

April shivered at the feel of his hands kneading and massaging her flesh before he lifted her with ease to wrap her legs around his waist as he backed them up to press her back against the cool glass of the sliding door leading to the balcony.

"Yes, yes, yes, oh, yes," she whispered as he

pulled her strapless top down to her waist, as well, and exposed her hard and throbbing nipples to his eyes, his hands and then his lips.

She closed her eyes and raised her hand above her head on the glass. She heard his fumblings with his belt even as he licked her nipples like they were ice cream. Seconds later he slid his hard penis up into her tight wetness with a one swift move that made them both cry out.

And they mated against the glass. The heat from their bodies fogging the window as they coupled as if they were starved. Grunts. Hard, fast and furious thrusts. Openmouthed kisses. Deafening heartbeats. Bites—some gentle, some not. Sweat. Urgency. Need.

They both cried out hoarsely with their shuddering releases as Lex dropped his head against the valley of her sweaty chest and April let her arms drop down to his shoulders.

"Your heart is beating so fast," he whispered against her cinnamon flesh.

"Think one of those high-society bitches would give you a little drive-by quickie like that?" she asked, her voice hard. "Or just a little ghetto girl like me?"

Lex lifted his head and looked at her with those blue-green eyes. "Don't, April," he warned.

"Let me down," she told him, her voice tired.

Lex stared at her for a long time.

April met his gaze unflinchingly, wondering what he was thinking.

Suddenly he stepped back from her, letting her down to her feet before he stepped back farther and roughly jerked up his pants, turning away from her.

"Men have women in these silly little groups. The ones you marry and take home to Mama and then the ones who aren't worthy to meet Mommy dearest, right? It's pretty clear what category I fall into…in your book anyway."

The truth shone in his eyes, and April only smiled sadly. "How dare you judge me? How dare you sit on your big white horse and look down on me. And why? Because I gave it up on the first night? Well so did you, Mr. Upper-Tenth Percentile. Because I don't cross the *t* and dot the *i* with my pronunciation? Because I'm not a Delta Sigma Omega Phi Gamma or whatever? Because my parents didn't bless me with intergenerational wealth? Because I'm not on a social register? Or I wasn't a debutante. Or is it because I can't pass the paper bag test? You and your kind still have that house slave versus field slave mentality."

Lex's jaw flexed and his eyes glittered. "And that's not judgmental, April? You can judge me and my life. You can look down your "woe is me" nose at me and that's okay? You're a hypocrite. You don't know me to make assumptions about me or my family."

April came to stand toe-to-toe with him. "And you don't know me, you...you...elitist. Maybe if I buy a Chanel suit and a string of pearls and talk like Hillary from like the *Fresh Prince of BelAir*, like your friends Tiffy and Lizzie, I'd like measure up."

"It's Tiffany and Lizzie. Do not bring my friends into this silly argument," he said in a hard voice as he glared down at her.

April's eyes widened. "You, Tiffy and Lizzie can go to hell together in a designer boat for all I care."

"If you don't care, why are you here?"

"I'm nobody's secret."

They glared at each other. Their chests heaved just as heavily from the arguing as they did from the sex.

"You know my brother-in-law, Maxwell, is a wealthy man. He has what your kind call 'new money,' but you could only wish to be half the man he is to his family, to his friends and to his *entire* community. You are a prime example of why class and wealth don't always go hand in hand. I don't know much about you but what little I know I ain't feeling one damn bit."

Lex threw his hands up in the air in frustration as he strolled away from her and then strolled back. "And that was my point exactly on why this sham of a marriage needs to be annulled. We don't know each other and have no business being married."

April crossed her arms over chest. "That will be remedied soon enough. Where are the annulment papers?"

He released a heavy breath. "At my office. I'll get them first thing in the morning."

The electrifying air between them began to die down as they both walked away from each other.

"I have enough manners to thank you for letting me spend the night until I fly out in the morning. I will sign the papers before I leave."

She walked to the door and then paused with the knob in her hand. "I would take back coming here if I could. It was a bad idea and childish and spiteful and wrong. I'm woman enough to admit that. I'm sorry, Lex. I just wanted to hurt you, and in the end I hurt myself."

April walked out of the study, tears already brimming in her eyes. Coming here was a mistake.

"Madame?"

April blinked rapidly and looked up to find a small, fine-boned brother dressed like The Penguin from *Batman* appear from nowhere. He was Lex's butler. "Are you everywhere?" she asked in disbelief.

"I try to be, madame."

"And what's your name again?"

"Sterling, madame."

"We's free now, brother," she told him conspiratorially.

He actually smiled and told her his annual salary without blinking an eye. "To tell you that is of course rude, madame, but I thought it necessary."

April looked impressed, and her eyes became mischievous. "Is he hiring for a maid? Hell, where can I get an ap? Can a sistah get down?"

Sterling actually laughed.

Lex pinched the bridge of his nose and flexed his shoulders to relieve the stress he felt tightening his muscles. *April.* His heart double pumped at the thought of her.

With reflective eyes he swiveled in his leather chair and looked at the spot on the sliding glass door where their bodies had made enough heat to make the glass sweat. Even now, hours later, his thick member stirred between his muscled thighs at the fiery memory.

Right now, knowing she was upstairs asleep in his home made him crave to crawl into bed beside her and cuddle her soft body to his while they slept. And knowing she would be gone in the morning saddened him deeply.

It was such a typical male thing. He wanted her but he didn't want to want her because she didn't fit into his world.

And now she would be gone and he was left to deal with picking up the pieces because she'd arrived and shattered his well-organized, predictable life.

Releasing a heavy breath, he looked down at the time on the tool bar of his open laptop. It was late. Almost eleven. His thoughts were too heavy to sleep.

"Do you need anything else before I retire, sir?"

Lex looked up in surprise to find Sterling standing in the doorway. "You didn't have to wait up for me, Sterling."

"No problem, sir."

"Well go on to bed. I've got some more things to work on."

Sterling nodded, but he remained standing there.

Lex looked up with questioning eyes.

"If I may, sir, Mrs. Macmillan has been crying nearly all night, sir. Perhaps you should check on her."

Lex frowned. "I'm the last person she wants to see."

Sterling nodded. "Perhaps, sir. Good night."

Lex leaned back in his chair and settled his strong chin against his fist. As badly as he wanted to climb the stairs and comfort April, he refrained. He already knew he couldn't stand to see her cry.

The next morning there was a knock at her door. April opened it to find her small carry-on suitcase sitting outside her door. She knew Sterling was responsible for that. When he showed her to one of the four guest suites in the two-level apartment, she had mentioned she left her suitcase at her hotel room.

She carried it inside the room to sit on the bed, unzipping it to withdraw undergarments and an outfit. Soon she would sign the papers to make her short marriage disappear and head back to Richmond to resume her life and pretend the last week had never existed.

Hard to think it had been just seven days since she first saw Lex on the elevator at the Bellagio.

April looked at her own reflection in the round mirror over the dresser and frowned a bit. Okay, meeting and marrying a man all within one week was insane.

He was right.

Hindsight was 20/20.

If she only knew then what she knew now.

Yadda, yadda, yadda.

"Bring on those dang papers," she muttered as she grabbed her toiletry kit and headed to her adjoining bathroom.

She was just emerging from the bathroom with a towel as thick as sin wrapped around her damp body when she heard a buzzer. She froze, only her eyes moving as they darted around the room. They eventually lit upon the intercom panel on the wall by the light dimmer. She walked over to it, still clutching her towel, and pushed the talk button. "Yes?"

"Good morning, Mrs. Macmillan. Would you care for breakfast?"

"Um, sure. Will Lex be eating as well?" she asked.

"No, madame, he's not home at the moment."

She flinched a bit. Couldn't even wait to tell me goodbye. But then she remembered he had to go to his office to retrieve the annulment papers. "Well, you don't have to bother just for me, Mr. Sterling."

"Just Sterling, madam. And no bother."

"I guess pancakes and bacon would be nice."

"Coming right up, madame."

At Gabby and Max's, whatever Addie cooked was all that was cooked. They either ate what she made or they didn't. No special requests. That was an Addie no-no.

She smiled when she thought of her family waiting for her back in Richmond. Gabby, Max, her nephew, Addie and Clayton. She was ready to get back to her life and put this all behind her. She had cried all the tears she had left last night. She got her revenge—no matter how much she regretted it—and now she wanted out of the marriage just as badly as Lex did.

April finished dressing in a white velour sweatsuit and then repacked her suitcase. She carried the small suitcase with her down the staircase, setting it by the base of the stairs.

"Your breakfast is ready, madame."

April looked at Sterling with an arched brow. Again he had appeared before he could even be summoned. "Are you psychic or just nosy?"

He smiled a little. "Right this way, Mrs. Macmillan."

"Oh no. It's April or Ms. Dutton."

"If you wish."

"I do."

He led her down a long corridor to the rear of the apartment. April had to admit that she loved Lex's home. The decor was contemporary and stylish in warm tones. It was obviously a man's home but one a woman could easily incorporate her own style into.

But that was a moot point with her. In a few hours her part in Lex's life would be even less significant than it was now. She would miss him—the fun they shared in Vegas—but she would be okay. She had no choice *but* to be okay.

He led her to an ornate dining room that held a table large enough to comfortably seat twelve. And there at the head was her lone place setting. April frowned as Sterling left her.

She promptly picked up her plate and her

silverware. She went out the door he'd walked through to find an elaborate kitchen that could rival that of a high-end restaurant. And there was an eating area with a huge fireplace, a sofa and a flat-screen television.

There was a male chef dressed in white stirring a pot on the stove as Sterling prepared her tray at a large marble island.

"Oh, Lord have mercy, a chef, too?" she asked.

"Good morning," the man greeted her, looking up from the sizzling pan on the Viking stove.

"And your name?" she asked.

"Eric Anthony."

"Well nice to meet you, Eric Anthony," she said.

"He was just finishing your breakfast. I will bring it to you," Sterling told her, looking up in surprise.

April sat at the huge island. "Give it to me right here," she said, setting her plate and silverware before her.

Sterling and Eric looked at her in amusement.

"Have you both eaten?" she asked as Sterling set some IHOP-looking pancakes and crisp bacon before her. "Come on and sit with me."

"That isn't proper, Mrs. Macmillan...Ms. Dutton."

She turned sideways and crossed her legs as she buttered each pancake. "I'm still Mrs. Macmillan for a minute," she said, not missing a beat.

They both looked at her in question. April cocked a brow and pointed her butter knife to Eric and then Sterling before pointing it toward the two stools at the island.

There wasn't a thing the two men could do *but* sit.

Lex entered his apartment, surprised when Sterling didn't appear within a few minutes. He saw the small carry-on sitting at the foot of the stairs. He frowned and flung the garment bags he carried over his shoulder as he strolled to the intercom to summon Sterling.

Moments later his trusted butler was standing at his side. "Good morning, sir."

"Morning, Sterling. Is Mrs. Macmillan up?" he asked, as he handed the butler the garment bags.

"*Mrs. Macmillan,* sir?"

Lex didn't miss the tinge of amusement in the butler's voice. "I meant Ms. Dutton."

"Of course you did, sir. And yes, sir, she's enjoying breakfast."

April strolled into the foyer, somehow looking angelic and sexy as sin in the white, fitted velour suit she wore. Lex found his eyes assessing her from head to toe. She still had the power to make him weak in the knees.

"Do you have the papers?" she asked.

"Sterling, will you take those bags to April's room? April, join me in the study."

She frowned.

He stopped in his path and turned. "Please," he stressed, waving his hand ahead of him as he looked at her.

April strolled into the study, turning to face him as she reached his desk.

Lex walked in behind her, closing the door before he moved to his desk in his black silk shirt and matching slacks. He put his briefcase on the desk and leaned back in his chair to study her.

April raised one shapely brow in question as she eyed him in return.

"I have a proposition for you, April," he began coolly.

"I doubt that there's anything I can do for you or you can do for me at this point, Lex."

His eyes shifted to the sliding glass door. "On the contrary," he told her dryly, shifting his eyes back to her. He didn't miss her shiver.

Yes, they still wanted each other. There was no denying that.

"Your surprise appearance leaves me in a bit of bind having to explain why the same woman who made a point of announcing our marriage to my family and friends at a private function is now gone the very next day."

He actually liked that April looked a bit uncomfortable. She wrote the check, now he wanted to see if she could cash it, as well.

"We both want the annulment, right?"

April looked unsure of his intent and it showed. "Yes, I'm Macy's and your Bergdorf. And your world is not one I want a part of. What's your point?"

"Stay here in New York until this dies down, and we get the annulment."

"Stay in New York? For what? No. I'm not staying in New York. I have my own life, my own friends and family in Richmond. No. No. Hell no."

Lex rose and came from around his desk to stand before her. He smelled her perfume. It was something sweet and tangy—just like the taste of her intimacy. A taste he remembered well.

"We both made a mistake with getting married in Vegas, but instead of quietly getting it annulled this whole situation has become anything but quiet." Lex turned and opened his briefcase, extracted a newspaper and turned back to hand it over to her.

April looked up at him before accepting the paper. It was opened to the society page. Her eyes widened as she read the blurb announcing that she and Alexander had announced their wedding last night.

"Damn, bad news travels fasts," she murmured.

"This isn't a joke, April," he roared, and then covered his mouth with his hand.

"I didn't say that it was, Lex," she countered.

"I am the CEO of a multimillion-dollar, high-profile business. I have over two thousand employees who rely on me to make the right decision at all times. My great-grandfather built up this company from a one-room office in Jersey City and my father handed it to me on a silver damn plate and like that—" he snapped his finger "—I risked it all. Do you understand how much pressure that is on me? Do you get what you have done with your payback?"

"My life is not ruled by society pages, Lex. Sorry." April leaned forward to drop the folded paper back into his open briefcase.

Lex walked to his desk and pulled open a drawer to extract a large billfold. He slapped it open to reveal blank checks. "How much?"

April shook her head as she looked at him. "Your kind always think people can be bought. There's not enough in your bank account, Mr. CEO, to make me do anything I don't want to do. I'm not for sale."

"You're right. I apologize for that." Lex nodded and closed the book, replacing it in the drawer. "Then I am asking as a favor to me, April. I need you."

"Keeping up an image is that important to you, Lex?"

He locked eyes with her. "Will you do this for me?" he asked, ignoring her question, the weight of his obligations figuratively weighing down his broad shoulders.

"Just give me the papers and let me go, Lex," she asked, sounding resigned and tired.

He extracted the papers from the briefcase and handed them and a Montblanc to her.

April didn't even look at him as she signed the document with flare where he indicated. She turned and walked out of the study. "Have a good life, Lex," she called over her shoulder, closing the door solidly behind her.

Chapter 7

Pillow Talk

April breathed deeply as she held on to the doorknob and leaned back against the study door. It had taken all the courage she had to sign those papers and walk away from Lex.

Yes, she'd talked a good game. She'd judged him and his world. She'd given a beautifully strong performance of being okay with the annulment, but the truth was, though she might not want the marriage, she still wanted the man. Badly.

Live here in this minicastle with the man she thought was going to be her very own Prince Charming? Too tempting.

April looked up at the stairs. She thought of the garment bags Lex had Sterling take upstairs. Curiosity won out. She jogged up the stairs and walked into the bedroom to find the garment bags laying on the bed.

Were they for her?

She moved to the bed and unzipped them all. There were at least a dozen outfits with shoes and matching purses. Some were a little conservative for her taste, but others suited her perfectly, especially the last one. She gasped in pleasure and lifted the dress from the bag to hold it up to the natural sunlight streaming through the bedroom window.

It was a beautiful creation by BCBG Max Azria. The stretch silk-charmeuse cocktail dress was so simple yet feminine and so trendy yet also classic with spaghetti straps and a full skirt.

It was exactly her style. April turned to close the bedroom door and carefully laid the dress down on the bed as she began to undress. She pulled the sequin stilettos and matching clutch from the bottom of the bag.

Once dressed, with her feet pressed into her

shoes, April studied the reflection. The cut and color of the dress fit her deep bronzed skin tone and her curvaceous body shape. All she needed was makeup and maybe twisting her hair into an up-do and she was all set to attend the wedding today with her husband.

It was obvious he had been banking on her staying on…for a little while anyway.

Regardless of her reasons why, and no matter how justified she felt her reasons were, her revenge tactic had put him in one hellified situation, whether she agreed or not about how he chose to live his life.

April opened her door and smiled to find her little carry-on case sitting there. She was on her way to seek out Lex, but she pulled it inside instead and took her time applying her make-up and jazzing up her hair.

When she was done, she studied her reflection. It was hard to escape the truth when it was staring you in the face. And the truth was she wasn't quite ready to have Lex gone from her life for good. Not quite ready at all. Marriage or no marriage, they shared a good time in Vegas. And now that they were on the same page about their marriage, some of her anger at him—some but not all—had dissipated.

April left her room again and carefully descended the stairs. Lex was just walking out of his study when he looked and caught sight of her. Her heart raced at the look on his face. It was the look of a man completely awestruck by a woman.

He held out his hand to her as she reached the bottom step. "The dress looks even better on you than I imagined it would, April."

Her hand burned from his light grasp. "Did you pick it out yourself?" she asked softly.

He nodded, as if he was at a loss for words.

"It's perfect," she admitted to him quietly, looking up into his eyes. Am I a fool to want him so badly—to want to be with him so badly?

"One month. Separate rooms."

Lex considered that. "Deal. It's not much, but it beats a blank."

April smiled. "Yes, it does, but it's the least I can do. Do you think it will work? I mean eventually we will get the annulment and you'll have to explain."

"Around these parts, one scandal tops the next pretty quickly. Just as long as they don't know we've only known each other a week."

April nodded. "My sister wasn't too happy about the news."

"You told her?" he asked in disbelief.

April nodded. "We tell each other everything. That's what family is for."

"I'm going up to get dressed," Lex told her, lightly kissing the back of the hand he still held. He jogged up the stairs and stopped midway to turn and look down at her. "Separate rooms, huh?"

April put her hand on her hip. "It could be separate states," she told him with a "don't play with me" look.

"Good point." Lex continued up the stairs, his laughter filtering down to her.

Sterling appeared. "If I may say, Mrs. Macmillan, look you beautiful," he said with a fatherly wink.

"'Mrs. Macmillan' just for a little while more, Sterling." April looked around her. This was her home for the next month. "What on earth have I gotten myself into?" she asked him.

"It may just be the best thing ever."

April looked doubtful.

Lex pulled his car into the parking lot of the Abyssinia Baptist Church. He looked over at April, his wife. He thought of their wedding and how he had truly in that moment wanted this woman in his life for the rest of his life.

He reached in his pocket and pulled out the Van Cleef box. "Give me your hand," he instructed as he removed the ring from the suede box.

April looked down in surprise as he slipped a platinum band with a weighty diamond on her left hand. "Wow, it's beautiful," she sighed holding her hand up to let the sunlight hit the stone. "Three carats?"

"Four," he told her as he opened his door and the seat belt automatically rolled from across his chest. He left the vehicle and came around to open April's door and hold his hand out to her.

"Thank you," she said, wiggling her fingers. "This plus the bold-faced lie—I mean story we came up with—should do the trick."

"It's an exaggeration, because knowing you for years and eloping seems less crazy than knowing you and marrying in Vegas all in one week."

"Call it what you want. A lie is a lie," April said.

"Real funny," he drawled as they walked together into the church. "I'm going to find War and check on him. You'll be okay?"

April nodded. "Yeah, I'll just grab a seat. I'll be fine."

She watched him walk away. Damn shame for one man to be so fine, she thought.

"My son is quite a man."

Okay, here we go. April turned and faced her mother-in-law. "Yes. Yes, he is. How are you today, Mrs. Macmillan?"

"I'm well…considering."

"Well you look beautiful," April said with honesty about the lilac lace suit the woman wore with a matching silk hat tilted to the side, both perfectly accentuating her short silver hair.

"Thank you. So do you, dear."

"Lex actually picked it out, and I just love it."

Candice's blue-green eyes—which her son inherited—took April in from head to toe. "It's amazing that Lex knows your taste so well after knowing you such a short time."

April met the woman's hard assessing eyes and did not miss the criticism laced in her words. "Lex and I have known each other for years actually, so he knows me quite well."

"Are you from New York?"

"Savannah originally, then Richmond."

"What did you do in Richmond?"

"Worked hard every day of my life."

"Doing?"

"At the time Lex swept me off my feet and

told me he couldn't live without me I was an executive assistant."

"*Oh*...okay. What university did you graduate from?"

April was willing to expand the truth of her life with Lex but she would not present her life as anything but what it was. She was not ashamed of it and refused to be judged by this woman or anyone else. "I was too busy working a full-time job and raising my baby sister, Gabrielle, once our parents died. She's a graduate of the University of Richmond."

Candice frowned. "You *did* graduate high school?"

"No, me don' know not'in' 'bout no learnin'," April said in a slow, docile voice. This woman was grating her nerves.

"That's not at all funny, dear," Candice chastised.

Big Mac walked up and wrapped his arm around his wife's waist as he leaned down to kiss April's cheek. "Hello, Ape."

Candice looked aghast. "Ape?"

"Ape is my nickname."

"My daughter-in-law told me to call her that at the restaurant last night."

"Ape?" Candice repeated in disbelief.

"That's me," April said with a Kool-Aid grin.

"Okay, ladies, let's go in and take our seat." Big Mac said, offering his free arm to April. "Of course, you're sitting with us."

"Of course, Big Mac," April told him with a genuine smile as she slipped her arm around his.

"Well, of course she is. Can you imagine what everyone would say if she didn't? Tongues are wagging enough, don't you think? I could just spank Alexander for this stunt."

April tried not to let them see her roll her eyes heavenward as they walked into the church and took their seats. She wondered just how long she could take Candice Macmillan before she gave her just what she was looking for—a good old-fashioned piece of her mind.

"Can you cook?" Big Mac whispered to her in the church.

"I can throw down and southern style, too. What do you like?" April whispered back.

"I haven't had something smothered in years."

"I got you."

"Good."

Candice leaned forward to glare at them both as the wedding began.

April squeezed her purse in between her

hip and the end of the church pew as she turned a bit in her seat as the first groomsman and bridesmaid strolled down the aisle together to "Ave Maria."

She had to admit that everything about the wedding said "proper." Images of War and Elizabeth played on an oversize projection screen above the altar. The decor and the floral arrangements were elegant and beautiful. The bridesmaids' deep red dresses were stylishly cut, and the perfect compliment to the groomsmen's crisp black tuxedos.

Lex and Tiffany were the last pair to walk the aisle. To April, the woman's hold around his arm was a little too firm, and the proximity of her body to his was just a tad too close. April studied them and had to admit that they made a handsome couple together. The perfect high-society couple.

As they neared her, April fought the childish urge to trip the woman. Tiffany gave April a satisfied smile as she lightly rubbed Lex's arm. Ignoring her, April shifted her eyes to her husband. She smiled to find him already looking at her. He winked and blew her a kiss, April lightheartedly caught it and then winked in return.

"Oh, heavens," she heard Candice say.

But April paid her no mind as she watched Lex's rear as he continued up the aisle. She wasn't going to lie that she was pleased when they finally reached the end and Lex went to stand beside War while Tiffany took her place as maid of honor on the opposite side of the aisle.

Everyone stood and turned to face the door as the bridal march began. The rear doors of the church opened and April heard the collective gasps as the bride made her first appearance, but April found herself looking over her shoulder. Her eyes sought Lex through the crowd and she was surprised to find his eyes on her, as well.

She thought of their own nuptials just a few days ago, and the event had not been this elaborate but at that moment—in the moment—it had been everything to her. He had been everything to her.

She dropped her gaze from his and looked down at the ring on her finger. *If only...*

Even as she reclaimed her seat and the wedding ceremony began, April thought of the last week of her life and the upcoming month. How had this man become so integral to her life? And why didn't she mind it one damn bit?

There was a collective gasp that shifted through the crowd like the wave at a football game. It caused April to look up. Her eyes landed directly on the projector screen where various erotic images of Elizabeth and another man played out. Each more daring and betraying than the last. In a few of the images the date and time was stamped at the bottom. Whoever played this cruel trick wanted everyone to know that it was just last night—the eve of their wedding day—that Elizabeth had betrayed War.

All hell broke loose just as the projection screen suddenly went black.

Nearly everyone jumped to their feet, blocking April's view of the altar as angry words mingled with pleading words echoed in the church. April stepped out into the aisle a bit just as Elizabeth dropped to the ground and grabbed War's leg as he attempted to walk away from her.

April frowned as the woman's rail-thin body was dragged a bit before he stopped, reached down and forcefully freed her hands. He walked away with his face like stone leaving her in a sobbing heap in the middle of the aisle. War pushed the double doors at the rear of the church with both of his hands causing them to slam forcefully against the wall as he strode out of the church.

Tiffany and the other bridesmaids stepped forward to help Elizabeth off the floor while her parents stood nearby exchanging words with War's parents. The minister was trying to restore order. Lex strode past Elizabeth to leave the church, as well.

April followed him.

She found him standing in the middle of the church parking lot. "He's gone, isn't he?" she asked as she lightly touched his arm.

Lex wiped his mouth and frowned. "Can't say that I blame him."

"It was quite a sight, that's for sure," April added lightly. "She's quite flexible."

Lex gave her a hard stare.

"What?" April asked with innocence. "I feel for War but it's good he knows the real deal about Miss Goody Two-Shoes. Maybe now he—and other people I know—will stop putting *certain* women on a pedestal."

"Not now, April."

"You're right. I'm sorry. You're probably worried about your friend." April felt ashamed to use such an improper moment to make a point—a good point—but a bad time nonetheless.

"I don't know if I should go inside and do damage control or try to find him."

She saw the concern for his friend, and April reached for his hand. With her free hand she reached up to lightly turn his face so that he looked at her. The pain she saw in his eyes touched her deeply. "Go find your friend," she told him softly. "He is much more important than all of that...all of that drama in there."

He nodded slightly as he looked down at her.

April smiled a little and stroked his cheek.

"Would you mind if my parents took you home?" he asked.

"Go. I'm fine. Go."

Lex reached into his pocket for his keys, taking one of the keys off the ring. "I already told the front desk you were staying with me, so just show them your ID. And here's the key."

She accepted it from him, and their hands briefly touched. "Okay, see you later," she told him as they walked together to his vehicle. "And drive carefully."

"I will." Lex opened the car door and turned briefly to kiss her in the most natural way before getting behind the wheel.

April touched her fingers to her lips even as he pulled away with a brief honk of his horn. That whole exchange felt more like a God-honest married couple than two people faking the funk. It felt natural and it felt right.

She turned and walked back toward the church just as the doors opened. A tall, buff brother dressed like Shaft in all black walked out. April's mouth fell open. It was the same man in the pictures with Elizabeth. Her steps faltered, and she paused as she watched him calmly walk away from the chaos he created.

April walked to him, quickening her steps as he reached a purple lowrider. She lightly touched his arm, and he looked down at her. "Why did you do it?" she asked, as if she knew this man.

He turned and looked at her. "Because I thought she loved me. Payback is a bitch," he answered simply before climbing into his car and driving off.

April had fallen asleep on the couch waiting up for Lex to get home. She pulled her body up to a sitting position on the couch and stretched like a lazy cat. It was after midnight.

Releasing a heavy breath and an unstoppable yawn, still in her dress, she rose and picked up her empty coffee cup to carry to the kitchen. Sterling met her in the hall before she made it there.

"I'll take that, madame."

"Thank you, Sterling. Is Lex home yet?" she asked.

"Not yet, madame. I'm sure he's fine—"

Just then they both turned as the front door flew wide-open and the sound of Lex singing off-key filled the foyer. Both April and Sterling stepped forward as Reginald, the chauffeur, assisted Lex into the apartment with obvious strain. April stepped aside as Sterling moved to help.

Lex looked up and saw April. He smiled. "There's my beautiful wife. My beautiful, beautiful wife."

April frowned and had to step back from the smell of liquor on his breath. "Take him up to his room," April told the men, easily falling into the role of the lady of the house.

She jogged ahead of them and moved into Lex's master suite. She paused in the doorway. This was her first look at it. Everything was tastefully and modernly decorated in shades of chocolate, khaki and ivory. There was a king-size bed, a full-size sitting room complete with a fully stocked bar and flat-screen television, and a open door revealed a walk-in closet just as big as the sitting room.

She moved forward into the room. The faint scent of his cologne—something subtle, masculine and intriguing—still hung in the air. There was an open book on the chocolate leather club chair in the corner. She picked it up and read the title. *The Covenant with Black America.*

She was impressed that he was reading it. It was on her own TBR—to be read—pile. She set it back down. Knowing she was wrong for snooping, she purposefully moved to the bed. She could hear the crispness of the sheets as she folded the covers down.

The gentlemen entered the suite with Lex still barely on his feet between them just as she noticed the photo on his bedside table. She gasped a little in surprise at the photo they'd had taken at The Venetian in Vegas. The night of their first date.

"War and I got f'ed up, April," Lex said, his voice slowing down as the men sat him on the edge of the bed.

"As a matter of fact, Mr. Kinsey is downstairs in the limo in the same condition. I should be getting him home, as well," the chauffeur said.

"Thank you, Reginald," April said, already kneeling to remove Lex's shoes as Sterling removed his tuxedo jacket.

"April. April. April. A-pril. April."

"What, Lex? What?" she asked in exasperation, looking up at him with only mild annoyance.

"It feels good to know when I come home you're here," he told her, his eyelids already heavy as he reached out and touched her face, his hand dropping a bit and catching on her bottom lip before it fell back to his side.

April rolled her eyes and yanked off his socks.

"April. April. April. April. April."

She looked over at Sterling who looked amused. "Yes, Lex?" she said with patience as her eyes shifted to him.

"Elizabeth's a no-good, dirty bit—"

"Yes, she is, Lex."

"Guess what I told War?"

"What?"

"I told him to sue her ass..."

"Stand up, Lex," April instructed him as she undid his belt.

Sterling assisted him to his feet, and the black pants fell easily around his bare feet.

"You wouldn't do that to me. Would you, Ape?" he asked, as he slumped back down onto the bed.

"No, I sure wouldn't." She pushed him onto his back.

"Not in front of Sterling," he whispered loudly.

Sterling bit back a laugh, and April put her hands on her hips. "Boy, don't play with me."

They finally got him settled under the covers. "April. April. April."

She stood at the side of his bed. "Yes, Lex."

"You got some good pus—"

"Lex," she shouted, cutting him off, and actually embarrassed to even look at Sterling who busied himself gathering up Lex's tuxedo.

He reached out for her wrist and looked up at her. "April, I love your ass. I do. I love you."

Her heart raced because even though they were married, that was the first time Lex had said he loved her. Not her dream scenario.

"Now I know you drunk."

He flipped his head to Sterling. "I love her, Sterling."

Seconds later he was snoring.

"Nothing worse than a drunk man or a sick man, either way they revert to being a child," April said. "Just rambling out of his head."

"Yes, but a drunk tongue speaks a sober mind, Mrs. Macmillan," Sterling said just before leaving the room and closing the door behind him.

April reached out to turn off the night lamp, but she paused with her hand on the tiny knob as she looked down at him. Even in a drunken stupor he was cute. She smiled a little and shook her head as she allowed herself one small press of her lips to his brow.

As she turned off the light and left the room, she wondered if he would remember any of what he said tonight. She knew she had every intention of trying to forget it.

Chapter 8

Woman to Woman

"I can't believe I'm wearing *this,* Lex."

"Why not, April? It's like playing dress-up."

"It's uncomfortable."

"You won't have it on for long. I promise."

"I'd rather be naked than wear it, Lex."

"Well, if you insist…"

"Whatever."

The elevator doors slid open and Lex held out his hand. "You look lovely, April," he said in her ear as she walked past him.

She looked down at the black pantsuit she wore and then looked up at him. "Nothing about this wool monstrosity says sexy. And trust, April Dutton likes to feel and to look sexy. You remember it's that same kind of sexy that caught your eye in Vegas. I don't recall any complaints about my wardrobe *then.*"

"You weren't having lunch with my parents then."

"I said sexy, not sleazy."

"The line is thin."

April swallowed her annoyance as they entered the apartment. "You and your parents can kiss—"

"Alexander!"

Lex's frown turned to a smile as his mother breezed up to him in a flowing multicolored silk caftan and pulled him down to her for a brief kiss on both of his cheeks. "Good afternoon, Mother."

While Candice fussed over Lex as if she hadn't just seen him yesterday, April took in the splendor and opulence of the apartment. Lex's was nice—it was better than nice—but this place made his look like a one-bedroom studio with discount furniture in comparison.

No wonder they keep their noses in the air. I can see why they think they're all that.

"April, you look pretty, dear," Candice said, moving forward to lightly kiss the air near April's cheek. April did the same.

"Thanks," April said, smiling as Candice led them into a living room that could rival a five-star hotel.

"Where's Daddy?" Lex asked.

"In the screening room watching a movie. Why don't you go talk business and leave us ladies alone," Candice suggested.

April took her seat and stiffened her spine, knowing the interrogation was about to continue.

"I'll just hang out with my two favorite ladies, if that's okay," he offered.

"No, Lex, we ladies are fine. Go talk to your father," April offered, a smile on her face as she locked eyes with Candice. Those eyes that said, "I'm not afraid of you."

Lex leaned over to whisper in April's ear. "Trust me, this may get ugly."

"Trust me, it's too late for that," April said, her smile never faltering. She patted his knee. "Go on. Get."

Lex rose, kissing April's cheek lightly before he left the room.

April went on the offense. "Mrs. Macmillan, it's obvious you have something you want to say to me or ask me. I don't have a problem with that."

"Okay, fine. Then let me lay my thoughts right out there for you. I am not at all happy about this spur-of-the-moment marriage. As a mother I am concerned about my son."

"Understandable."

"It is not at all a part of the plan his father and I had...*have* for him."

"Plans for a thirty-year-old man. That's quite presumptuous of you."

Candice smiled but it didn't reach her eyes. "A *successful* thirty-year-old man, and a large part of that is due to the life his father and I prepared for him."

April nodded and crossed her legs as she settled back against the sofa. "You should be commended for the foundation you've laid, but give him credit for his personal sacrifices that contribute to his own success as well, Mrs. Macmillan."

"I have nothing but respect for my son."

"That's good to know. Perhaps you should convey that to him."

Candice rose and walked around the ornate living room. "This all must be a little overwhelming for you, April."

April frowned. "What do you mean?"

"The wealth and the status of this family." Candice waved her hand around the room. "We are well respected in our community."

"I guess that's good if that's what is of importance to your family

"It comes with the territory, dear."

Meaning: your broke-ass family don't know jack 'bout living with money. "Not always," April responded.

The woman had the audacity to laugh. "How would you know, dear?"

Her tone was just condescending enough to make April have to count to ten. And during that count she refrained from bragging about her wealthy but down to earth brother-in-law. It was unnecessary because April had no desire to impress this woman.

"What I do know is that not once, in these little tête-à-têtes of ours have you talked about him being happy. Or even asked me what I plan to do to *keep* him happy? Or better yet, if

I love him? If I respect him? Cherish him? Need him?" April spoke with conviction as she counted her list off on her fingers. "Do I promise to uplift him? Promise to support him? Will I be faithful and loyal? Will I spend the rest of my life with him? Build a family with him? Isn't that what's important?"

Brrrnnnggg.

"You're sweet, dear," she said, before walking over to pick up the phone.

April didn't even try to hide her exasperated eye roll. Lord, this woman can work a nerve. No wonder Lex got issues.

"Let her up," Candice said into the phone before hanging it up. "That's Tiffany. I invited her to have dinner with us."

April forced a smile, quite sure that Candice wanted Tiffany to have way more than dinner.

Namely Lex.

"Would you like something to drink, son?"

Lex frowned. "No, War and I did enough of that yesterday and I am still feeling the effects."

Big Mac lit a fat cigar as he sat forward in one of the twenty leather movie-theater-style chairs. "How's he doing?" he asked, sending his son a sidelong glance.

"He was pretty tore up yesterday." Lex leaned back in his own chair, making it recline. "I can't believe Elizabeth would cheat on him."

"I don't know why you don't believe it, with all that evidence we *all* saw yesterday," Big Mac barked as he picked up the remote and turned down the volume on the movie screen.

"That was a side of Lizzie I didn't need to see." Lex dropped his head against the plush back of the chair.

"Your mother put her hands over my eyes."

"I really thought War and Lizzie would have a real marriage."

"Unlike yours with Ape?" Big Mac asked as he made smoke rings.

Lex realized his slip. "I just meant they did everything the right way. The dating. The intros to family. The engagement. The big wedding."

"If that's how you feel, why didn't you wait, son?"

Lex thought of the week he spent with April in Vegas. How alive and happy he felt just spending time with her. Making love to her. Sleeping with her in his arms. And then he thought of that last night as they stood before the fountains and how the thought of never seeing her again had pained him.

"Because I felt like I couldn't live the rest of my life without her," he answered with honesty. "And that moment I wanted her to be my wife. And all the society crap and putting on a big showy wedding didn't matter one damn bit."

Big Mac smiled at his son. "You mother wants me to grill you about Ape. And I won't say that I wasn't a bit nervous and filled with my own questions about all of this. For a minute I though you lost your mind, but if you both have known each other for some time—whether we've met her or not—and decided to be spontaneous and elope then I'm willing to let you be a man and make your own decision."

Lex felt a bit of guilt for the lie he and April came up with.

"As long as this doesn't affect your ability to run the business and maintain its successfulness, then *for me* your personal business is your personal business, son."

And there was the subtle reminder of his responsibilities and his obligations. No, his father was never overbearing when it came to his personal life, but the business was always a priority. Not that Lex could blame him. Still, it was the total success or failure of the business being lumped onto his lap that was overwhelming.

"Besides, if Ape's smothered pork chops are as good as she says, then she's really good to go."

Lex just smiled because he didn't have a clue if April could cook or not.

"Now, your mother is another matter."

"True."

"She's probably grilling the poor girl about lineage and all that. Let's go save her."

Lex rose from his chair. "April can handle herself, but you're right, let's go get her."

Candice left April and Tiffany alone to go and check on dinner. The two women sat across from each other, intermittently ignoring each other with stony silence or shooting each other hard stares filled with dislike.

April was particularly annoyed that the pantsuit Lex asked her to wear today was almost identical to the pastel suit Tiffany wore. She couldn't wait to give Lex a piece of her mind about *that.* She didn't give two hoots if she did agree to help him. She refused to be made into a Tiffany clone.

"You know, April, it's odd that Alexander never mentioned you, since he and I have been friends for ages. I wonder why he kept you such a secret?" Tiffany asked, looking smug.

"Now that I've met you I have no doubt why Lex failed to mention *you.*"

"You little hood rat!" Tiffany gasped as she slid to the edge of her chair.

"You snobby slut," April countered, sliding to the edge of her seat, as well.

"You know nothing about me."

April cocked a sassy brow. "I know birds of a feather flock together, and yesterday we all saw that your buddy is a quite a pro at being a ho."

Tiffany rose. "If you think I'm scared of you you're wrong."

April sighed like she was bored. She sat back in her chair, crossed her legs again and studied her nails. "I'd hate to break a nail snatching that silky, stupid looking weave off your head."

Tiffany touched her hair as she scowled at April. "This is *not* a weave."

"Girl, please, *white* women's hair ain't *that* shiny."

Tiffany rose to her feet.

April rose to hers.

"What on earth does Lex see in you?"

"Obviously something he didn't see in you."

April brushed her bangs out of her face with her left hand showing off the rock.

"You're not even on our level," Tiffany spat.

"Look here—woman to woman—if you believe that I'm not the woman for Lex and you are, then go for it. I am past that stage in my life where I will argue and fight another woman over a man. That's high school."

Tiffany smiled cattily. "I will have Alexander."

April stopped herself from dropping another snide comment. Why argue over Lex? In a month's time—if she could make it *that* long—she would be back in Richmond and her marriage would be legally nonexistent.

So Tiffany could very well be right about her having Lex.

"I'm going to find Lex," April said, turning to leave the room.

"Mrs. Macmillan wants you gone just as badly as I do."

April paused in the doorway and looked over her shoulder at the woman. "Too bad for you both that it's not up to either of you."

"I wouldn't be so sure of that."

April turned fully and walked back to Tiffany with long strides. "See, you can't be mature and grown-up with silly bitches like you."

"Hey, Tiff," Lex said strolling into the living room.

And like that, the woman's face changed from angry and combative to sweet as can be. "Hello, Alexander," she said, brushing past April to wrap her arms around his neck as she pressed her body to his.

April licked her lips and fought the childish urge to yank the woman by her hair.

He used his hands on her waist to set her away from him a bit, before moving to stand beside April and wrap his arm around her waist. "Dinner's ready. We better go on to the dining room."

April loved the comfortable feel of Lex's hand on her back as they moved through the foyer and into the dining room. But she made herself tune it out as she quickly went to Big Mac's side to kiss his cheek in greeting before moving back to Lex.

"Have you talked to Lizzie?" Lex asked as he held first April's seat and then Tiffany's.

Tiffany nodded. "She's a mess, and she's torn because Warrick won't talk to her or let her explain. Maybe you could talk to him, Lex. I think it's a big misunderstanding, don't you?"

April watched Candice and Big Mac exchange a look as the servers brought out their food.

She felt Lex's body tense up beside her. "I don't know. We're all friends, so I don't want to take sides, but right now War is the victim in all this. Still, I know we're all human and we all make bad decisions, so I would never turn my back on Lizzie."

"Yes, but Lizzie loves Warrick."

Big Mac snorted in disbelief, earning him a hard stare from his wife.

"Maybe it was a one-night stand," Tiffany protested.

"It wasn't." April said before swallowing a spoonful of the delicious broccoli-and-cheese soup.

She felt all eyes on her.

"How would you know?" Tiffany asked with attitude.

Candice waved her hand dismissively. "There's no way she could know."

April shrugged in nonchalance. "This soup is delicious," she said to Big Mac.

"Good as your smothered pork chops?" he asked with mischievous eyes.

"No way. Trust."

"April!"

She turned and look at Mrs. Macmillan. "Yes?"

Candice looked heavenward and dropped her napkin onto the table. "My word."

"Baby," Lex began, reaching for her hand.

She turned to him. "Yes?"

He licked his lips to keep from smiling. "Why did you say it wasn't a one-night stand?"

"Because I saw him leaving the church after you left to go find War."

"That bastard came to the church!" Lex roared, pushing his bowl away in anger.

"Alexander Macmillan," Candice said in reprimand.

"He probably came to see his handiwork. I mean who else put the film in the projection screen anyway," Big Mac offered. "I'd have to agree with Ape. Doesn't sound like a one-night stand to me."

April's eyes went to Tiffany who was decidedly quiet during the whole exchange. "Tiffany, I thought Elizabeth was staying with you that night before the wedding. Did she sneak out to get her freak on?" April asked with feigned innocence. "You didn't know she wasn't at your place. Or did it happen at your place?"

"It most certainly did not." All eyes rested on

Tiffany. When the stares did not falter, she added, "I'm just as surprised as the rest of you."

Yeah, okay, whatever. Tiffany knew all about it, but she was smart to keep her nose and her ass out of the line of fire. Still, April felt a little pleased that everyone at the table looked doubtful of her ignorance about her best friend's undercover lover.

Chapter 9

I Was Made for You

"What's wrong, April?" Lex asked her for what seemed the hundredth time since they left his parent's home.

"Nothing's wrong, Lex," she stressed as she looked out the window of his Benz. I just dislike your mother big-time, but other than that, I'm cool.

His cell phone began to ring and he reached for it on the console of his car. "Lex Macmillan…oh, hey, War. What's up, man?"

April reached into her purse for her own cell phone and quickly checked her voice mail.

There were two messages from Gabby and one from Clayton telling her that Raoul was actually in Richmond for a week. She'd call them tonight when she was in her room.

"Okay, War. Well, call me if you need anything."

April's eyes shifted over to him once he placed the phone back on the console. "How's he doing?"

Lex shook his head as he briefly glanced over at her. "He's doing better. Elizabeth is blowing up his phone and stalking him a little bit. He's actually going away for a while. No one knows but me."

"Not even his parents?" she asked, surprised by that.

"Nope, they actually want him to reconcile with Elizabeth. He's going up to this cabin we have in the mountains." Lex slowed the car to a stop at a red light.

"I hope it helps him get through this all."

"Thank you, April."

"Well, he means something to you, so he means something to me."

Damn. What was she saying?

Lex reached over and gathered her hand into his as if it was the most natural thing in the world.

And they continued to hold hands even as they rode the elevator upstairs to the apartment, talking about their plans for the day ahead.

"What will you do all day while I'm at work?" Lex asked as they walked into the foyer of the apartment together.

"I am going to enjoy New York to its fullest and I think I'm going to make those smothered pork chops for your dad."

"Just my dad?" he asked in amusement, his blue-green eyes twinkling as he looked down at her.

"You have a chef."

"So does he," Lex said, as he pulled her behind him into the living room.

And she let herself be led. "You just want me to cook for you," she said, as he opened the screen door and led her onto the balcony.

"True."

"Oh my God," April sighed. "What a sight."

The New York cityscape was awesome. Somehow the blackness of night and the brilliance of millions of lights coexisted to make a postcard-worthy view. And that moved April, because for each tiny light there was a life, a family, a story, and it intrigued her that there were so many many lights.

"I know. It's amazing. Sometimes if I find the time to enjoy it I can sit out here all night."

Lex stood beside her on the balcony and April looked over at him. "It must become *when* I make time and not if. Life's too short."

"That's easier said than done," Lex said, his deep and masculine voice sounding almost regretful about that.

"It's easier than you think, Lex."

They fell silent and just enjoyed the view and the quiet comfort of each other's company.

April smiled as she thought of his drunken actions last night: the singing, the need to be nearly carried to his bedroom and undressed, the declaration of love.

"I can't believe it's only been a week since I first saw you on that elevator," April said. "Just eight days."

Lex released her hand to put his arm around her shoulders and hug her close to his side. "I remember seeing you and thinking how sexy you are. Way sexier and more alluring than all the strippers we'd seen—"

April elbowed his side lightly. "Well, thank God for small favors, Alexander Macmillan."

He chuckled. "What did you think when you first saw me?" he asked.

"Wanting your ego stroked?"

"Perhaps."

April pretended to think about it. "I remember saying he's fine, but I don't fool up with high-yellow men."

"I can't tell."

April looked up at him. "You looked hungry that night on the elevator so I invited your red self to dinner. That's all."

Lex looked down at her. "Yes, but it was you I ended up eating that night."

April flushed with warmth. "And quite well."

Lex looked down at her and she looked up at him.

"We shouldn't be doing this," he said, his head already lowering as he raised his hands to her face.

"What?"

"This." Lex sucked April's mouth whole before he gently probed her lips open with his tongue.

April's hands rose to his waist to grip his shirt as she tilted her head back and gave in to his kiss filled with passion and want. When Lex scooped her up into his arms, she sighed in contentment, allowing him to carry her through his study and up the stairs to his bedroom as she nuzzled his neck with her lips like it was the most natural thing in the world.

As he pressed her body down into the plush softness of the bed, none of their differences or their issues mattered.

Mama was a snooty bitch. *Who cares.*

April fell below the social radar. *So what.*

He made her annual salary in a day. *And?*

He let high society's rules rule his life. *He wasn't the first and wouldn't be the last.*

They put an expiration date on their marriage. *It's what we both want. We'll be okay.*

April sighed as Lex began to undress her with slow ease in the darkness of his bedroom. She gasped with every touch of his capable hands to her flesh. She moaned with every press of his soft lips to her quivering body.

Lex worked his way down every delicious curve of her body—her skin as smooth as silk. He opened her legs before him and lowered his head to the sweet, heated vee between her thick thighs. He inhaled her unique scent and felt his shaft press with steely strength against the zipper of his pants. Feeling restricted, he rose from her heated and writhing body long enough to strip until he was as naked as she.

At the first connection of his body pressed deeply against hers, they gasped as if electrocuted.

"Slow it down," he whispered against her face as his arms wrapped tightly around her. He kissed her cheek as they both breathed slow and easy.

"Yes," April whispered as they began to massage each other's body. "Yes."

Lex began to plant tiny kisses—dozens of them—over her face and chin before he lightly pressed his lips down upon hers. His hands rose to hold her face, and April brought hers up to do the same to his. They shared those comfortably intimate kisses filled with sexy familiarity as tiny pecks deepened to languid and sensual kisses that seemed to last for hours.

Even as April opened her legs wide and wrapped them around his back as Lex slid as much of his lengthy hardness as he could into her slick, wet core they kissed. Their moans of pleasures were swallowed into open mouths as they shivered and their hearts raced.

"Don't move, baby," he whispered tightly,

pressing his face into her neck as he struggled for control.

April let her hands explore the strong contours of his shoulders, his back and his firm buttocks as Lex finally began to grind his hips ending each rotation with a deep pump that caused April to holler out...each and every time.

He shifted his hands down her body to firmly grasp her buttocks as he deepened, strengthened and increased the speed of each stroke until he was like a well-oiled machine working her.

April bit her bottom lip and arched her back. "Oh, that feels good," she gasped, tightening her grasp of his buttocks and enjoying the way they vibrated in her hands as he sexed her.

"Put your legs down," he instructed her throatily, raising his entire body up so that she could. "Now close them."

April lightly smacked his bottom as she pressed her legs closed beneath him. "Like that?" she whispered into his ear, lightly licking the lobe and enjoying the shiver she caused.

Lex kissed his way up from her neck to her lips. "Now pop it."

April stroked his buttocks once last time before moving her hands up to his shoulders as she suckled his tongue deep into her mouth and began to work her hips up and down. The tightness of her walls pressing against his steely rod caused them both to holler out roughly.

"Nice and slow," Lex moaned against her mouth. "We got nothing but time, baby."

April kissed Lex and worked her hips in a slow, snakelike, rhythmic motion that was erotic.

"Damn, April...damn."

Lex rose up enough to suckle one taut nipple into his mouth as she continued to grind. His tongue flickered the thick nipple as he began to grind back.

"I love when you suck my nipples," she said huskily, lightly biting her tongue as she arched her back some more—never once stopping that wicked circular grind of her hips.

"You do?" he asked, slightly cocky.

She nodded, raising one hand to press to the back of his soft head as she purred like a well-stroked kitten—or was it because her kitten was being stroked well?

They made love in perfect unison, bringing each other intensified pleasure like that was their sole purpose for even being alive. To please and be pleased by that one person in the world made just for them.

With his long and thick rod still planted deep within her moist core, Lex put each of April's legs on his shoulders. He then leaned down until her knees were nearly to her ears. Thank heaven, I'm flexible. "Wow, that feels good."

"Yeah?" Lex asked, pushing another inch inside of her.

"Ohh. Oh, yes."

Lex reached over to the left.

"What are you doing?" April asked.

He turned on the bedside lamp and looked down at her. "I want to see your face when I make you come."

That turned April on and she felt her core warm, moisten and throb even more.

Lex smiled. He felt it, too.

April buried her face against his chest.

Lex laughed a little.

April plopped her head back on the pillow to glare up at him. She was very tongue-in-cheek as she began to work the muscles of her vagina against his stiffness with a deadpan, serious face.

Lex's smile fell and his sexy blue-green eyes smoldered. "Girl, you...are...bad," he said in reverence.

"Now *I'll* watch your face while *I* make you come," she told him in a soft tone that was still cocky and bold as she continued to work her interior muscles, pulling him deeper into her core and then releasing him in a fluid one-two motion that made him harder. She felt it.

"Well I'll be damned," he said, his voice amazed as he lay still and enjoyed the way she worked her vaginal muscles without moving her body.

He kissed her briefly as he stared down into her eyes. "I'm going to come," he gasped.

April licked her lips, tilted her head to the side and arched a brow. "I know," she told him cockily.

Lex flung his head back and lifted himself to his elbows to stroke deep within her as he came deep inside of her.

"Yes," April screamed roughly, closing her eyes as he pumped away, his hard shaft hitting her G-spot until she joined him in climaxing.

He lay down to wrap his arms around her tightly, and she held on to him as well. The sweat from their bodies slickened the last furious moments of their lovemaking as they both cried out roughly from each mind-blowing spasm that drained them of their releases and sent them to a world where nothing existed or mattered but the two of them in that moment.

* * *

April awakened the next morning—in Lex's bed—with a stretch. She had had every intention of going back to her own room last night, but the last thing she remembered was Lex kissing her as his arm held her body tightly against his.

She must have fallen right into a deep sleep.

"Oh, Mrs. Macmillan."

April looked up at Sterling standing in the doorway with clean linens in his arms. "Morning, Sterling."

"I had no idea you were in here, madame."

"Well, it wasn't on my to-do list, either." April thanked the heavens the sheet was covering her body as she kept it wrapped around her and rose from the bed.

"A good night, madame?" Sterling asked with a hint of smile at his lips.

April walked past him to leave the room. "I have no idea what you mean."

"Um, madame?"

April turned in the doorway to look at him.

"Your thong," he said, picking it up off the floor to hand to her.

April walked to him without looking in his eyes and snatched it from him.

"I'll gather up all your other clothing and have them laundered."

"Thank you," April said over her shoulder as she left the room and hurried down the hall to enter her own.

Once the door was closed, she actually laughed.

After a quick shower, April pulled her last clean outfit from her small suitcase. It was more casual then the clothes Lex had purchased for her to wear. She pulled on the tiered, beaded skirt in shades of navy, turquoise and white with a white cami and a fitted denim jacket. Once dressed she went in search of her pocketbook.

She found it in the study where she'd left it last night. She sat on the leather couch and pulled out her cell phone to call her sister.

"Hey, you."

"Ape? I thought you were headed home yesterday. What happened?" Gabby asked, the sounds of Max playing with the baby in the background.

"Well, I wasn't exactly honest to you about why I came to New York," April said, looking out the sliding glass door to the tops of the towering buildings across from them.

"O-okay. Okay. Well, fill me in."

And as she had so many times in the past with her usual man-drama, April told her sister *everything.*

"Ape, what on earth were you thinking crashing a private dinner and announcing a marriage neither one of you had any intention of continuing?"

"I know, Gabby." April's eyes went to the sliding glass door and she flushed at the memory of the great sex they shared as he pressed her body into it.

"So now you're staying there at his apartment?"

"His beautiful, beautiful apartment," April emphasized. "He has a butler and a part-time chef and he has celebrity neighbors. I'm on the look-out for Diddy. Trust."

"April, have you lost your mind?"

"No. Yes. No. I don't know." She began to bite her thumbnail in earnest.

"Do you know how long you're staying there?"

"Just long enough to feed his parents the story about us dating on and off for years and eloping."

"Maybe you two are meant for each other 'cause both y'all crazy as two left shoes to think that's gon' work. Aren't you still getting the annulment?"

"Yes."

"But you two are screwing like rabbits in the meantime."

"Yeah. Girl, I did my little trick on him with my—"

Gabby sighed heavily. "Max, give me the baby. You talk to her. I'm about to scream."

Seconds later Max was on the phone. "Hey brother-in-law."

"Hey to you. Are you drinking?"

"No."

"Are you high?"

"Hell, no."

"Are you in your right mind?"

"Yes." April frowned in confusion. "I know I still owe you the money."

"I'm not worrying about that."

"Oh, okay."

"Are you in danger?"

"No."

"Good. See you when you get back."

April dropped her head in her hands when she heard Gabby say, "Give me that phone. Have you lost your mind, too?"

"What?" Max asked.

Seconds later, Gabby was back on the phone. "April, you need to sign those papers and bring your butt back to Virginia with a quickness. The whole thing is insane."

"I'm fine, Gabby," April insisted.

"I want a phone number, address and your husband's full name."

April rolled her eyes but she gave Gabby the info. "He's not a killer. He was just on the cover of *Black Enterprise* magazine."

"Whoopee."

April smiled. "I gotta go."

"'Kay. And answer your cell phone."

"Love you, sis."

"Love you the same. Bye."

April ended the call and then dialed Clayton's cell phone and home number. Both went to voice mail. "Hi, Clayton. It's me, April, just calling to fill you in on the latest adventures and times of April Dutton. You're not going to believe this. Guess we're playing phone tag. Call me back on my cell because I'm in New York. Love you. Bye."

April slid her cell phone back into her hobo bag. It was then she noticed the note stuck in the outside pocket of her bag.

She opened the paper and a black American Express card fell onto her lap. Her brows rose as she picked it up. Lex's full name was stamped across the bottom.

The note read:

I thought you would need more clothes for the time you were in New York. And I admit that pantsuit did you no justice. I already told Sterling to donate it to charity. I drove to the office, so the driver is at your disposal today. Have fun shopping. Looking forward to dinner.

Lex

P.S. Please don't think this is payment for services rendered. I know how your mind works.

April looked down at the card. "Maybe just a few things," she said. Why the hell not?

Lex dropped into the oversize leather executive chair behind his desk, leaning heavily into it as he took a well-deserved break from an entire day of meetings.

The intercom buzzed. He started to ignore it, but in his business ignoring a call or a visitor could cost him or one of his clients millions. He hit the button. "Yes, Amanda."

"Mrs. Macmillan's here to see you."

Some of the stress of the day that weighed his broad shoulders down lifted at the thought of seeing April. He actually smiled for the first time that day. "Send her in," he said, already rising from behind his desk to cross the wide expanse of his office to pull the door open for her.

"Hi, baby..." Lex's words trailed off at the sight of his mother.

Candice reached up to pat his masculine cheek as she strolled past him into the office. "Surprised to see me, dear?"

Lex hid his disappointment. "I thought it was April, but I am of course always happy to see you."

Candice took a seat before his desk.

He patted her shoulder as he moved to reclaim his seat. "How can I help you?"

"I actually wanted to talk to you about April."

Lex crossed his hands atop his desk. "Fire away."

"This is the first moment alone we've had since your *announcement.*"

Lex wasn't fooled for a minute by the small

talk. His mother was a woman on a mission. He remained quiet as he leaned back in his chair.

"I don't approve of this marriage."

"Why not?" he asked simply, bracing his square chin on his hand.

"She is not at all suitable to be a Macmillan."

"Because?"

Candice looked amazed. "I mean really, Alexander. That is a very silly question for you to ask."

"How can you judge a woman you know nothing about."

"Whose fault is that if I don't know her?" was Candice's retort. "You've known her for all these years and never once mentioned her or introduced her to the family until *after* you two elope. Hardly appropriate. I'm surprised at you, because I know you know better."

This was his mother being overbearing at level six on a scale of one to ten. If she knew he in fact had met and married April within one week, she would be ballistic. He just didn't have the time, the patience or the inclination to talk his mother off the ledge with that one.

We tell each other everything. That's what family is for.

April's words came to him. It was sad that he had to lie to his own mother to avoid disappointing her or having her judge him. "Did you have her sign a prenuptial?"

"That's a private matter between April and me, Mother." Lex picked up his pen and began to read and then initial several contracts on his desk.

"If you were itching to get married, why on earth would you overlook a wonderful woman like Tiffany?" Candice tapped the desk lightly to get his attention. "Tiffany, Lex, why not Tiffany?"

"Mother, Tiffany is my friend and she's not my type."

Candice laughed. "What is your type, cheap and uneducated?"

At that Lex felt anger—true anger—at his mother. "April is my wife, Mother, and that was completely disrespectful to me and to her. Disagree with our marriage. Disagree with my choice, but I respectfully ask that you not insult her again. It's uncalled for."

Candice sat back in her chair, clasped her hands atop her lap, and looked at her son for a long time. "That's a first, dear."

"Ma'am?" he said with all due respect.

"April's the first woman you've defended to me," she said, obviously surprised. "I don't know if that's a good or a bad thing."

"She's special," he said, immediately realizing he meant the words as soon as he spoke them.

He thought of her. Her smile. Her scent. Her ability to make him laugh and to relax and enjoy life.

"In fact," he said, looking down at his watch, "I'm going home early to enjoy the dinner she's making for me."

Lex rose and pulled on his tailored jacket. Candice rose, as well, sticking her clutch purse under her arm. "Don't let your…wife…make you forget your obligations to this business, Alexander."

He froze in putting important files into his briefcase. "I am well aware of my duties, Mother. I'm reminded quite often in fact."

Candice turned as she reached the door. "You sound annoyed with me."

"Can I drop you home, Mother?" he asked as they walked out of his office together.

"No, I have the limo."

Lex paused at his assistant's desk. "Amanda, I'm leaving for the day but I'll be working from home. If there's anything urgent just call me on my cell."

"An early day? Good for you, Mr. Macmillan." Amanda smiled up at him.

"If my wife calls tell her I'm on my way home."

"When will we get to meet her?" Amanda asked.

"Very soon. Good evening, Amanda."

Lex escorted his mother out the building, and his chest felt light with anticipation at seeing April. His wife.

With each passing moment it sounded more and more right.

Chapter 10

Kiss & Say Goodbye

April and Lex fell into a comfortable groove during the next two weeks. She had actually taken over cooking dinner for them both, and they spent quiet evenings reading together, talking or watching television.

They had ventured out once to attend an award banquet together, but that opened the floodgates in questioning their sudden marriage. They both decided it was best to lay low in the house, or the whole purpose of staying together just long enough for curiosity to wane was defeated.

April actually enjoyed their evenings together and was pleased when Sterling admitted that he had never seen Alexander so happy. Every single night he made a point of being home by at least seven—another first according to Sterling.

Although they shared explosive sex nightly, sometimes chasing each other around the big apartment before making love wherever they were caught, April insisted that she returned to her own bed to sleep. Lex wanted it otherwise but she held on to that preference.

It was her silly way of weaning herself from the man. And her even sillier way of stopping the hundred-mile-per-hour crash into falling deeper in love with him.

It wasn't very successful.

Lex was truly a good man—a good person—who wasn't afraid of being strong or weak when needed. He was intelligent. He was affectionate—he would hold her all night if she let him. He was reserved and quiet, but he allowed her to bring that funny side out of him until he laughed till he cried. He cherished his friends and called regularly to check on War. He was dignified, admitting to her his disdain for the strip clubs they'd attended in Vegas. He'd never been to one and had no plans to return to any…ever.

He was disciplined, immediately resuming his workout regime now that he was home more than he was at his office. And his work for the company never suffered as he bragged on their financial success at the end of the quarter. And he was romantic—even more so than he'd been in Vegas. Flowers. Massages. Gifts. Calls to say he was thinking of her.

Alexander Macmillan was making it very hard *not* to love him. Very hard indeed.

She was lying across her bed watching television when her cell phone's ring tone sounded. She sat up, her heart racing, as she looked around her for clarity.

The phone sounded again, and April reached for it. "Hello."

"What's up, stranger?"

April's face lit up at the sound of Clayton's deep voice. "Hey, you. How you doing?"

"I'm doing good. How's the Upper East Side treating you?" he asked, sounding amused.

"It's good as it can be considering the circumstance. You know I'll be coming back home in two more weeks."

"I still cannot believe your slick ass got married in Vegas and said not a word to me."

"I was too embarrassed about my marriage lasting less than a day. I think we were breaking Britney Spears's record. So it wasn't like it was good news."

"Still…"

April nodded, rising from the bed to enter the walk-in closet. "For the thousandth time in two weeks…forgive me. We cool?"

"Cool."

"Good because we have a dinner to go to tonight at his parents'—Lord help me—"

"Is his mother still playing the wicked witch?"

"The wicked witch with a Martha Stewart smile." April reached for a sheer black lace, short-sleeved top, black camisole and vintage jeans. "The last time we were there she laid out full place settings all the way down to shrimp forks. That woman is a mess."

"Never let her see you sweat, Ape."

"That's nothing. It's forever Etiquette 101 at the Macmillans'."

"A woman with not a bit of manners trying to quiz others on etiquette. Ironic." Clayton laughed, full, rich and deep, as though that truly tickled his funny bone. "What are you wearing?"

April explained her outfit to him.

"I love it. Top it with a few long gold necklaces, slip on some gold stilettos and you are good to go."

April nodded. "Sounds like a plan."

"I'll be glad when you're home."

"Me, too," April said.

"Liar," Clayton joked.

"Okay, truth?"

"Always."

"I'm enjoying being with him, but the sooner I get away the better because I feel myself falling for him." April sat down on the end of the bed.

"Falling? April, you already fell."

April lifted her head and looked at her reflection in the mirror over the dresser. The truth was hard to hide from yourself and from your good friends.

Yes, she loved him. *Of course* she loved him. And she had loved him ever since that first night in Vegas. It was time to stop denying it.

"You are so right, my friend."

"Surprise!"

April and Lex looked like deer caught in

headlights as they looked at the group of people assembled in the foyer of his parents' apartment. Lex felt April tense beside him, and he pressed his hand to the small of her back and massaged it, hoping to alleviate some of her stress.

Lex forced a smile to his face as his friends and family moved forward to greet him and April. This was of course his mother's doing, and of course to hell with the fact that he specifically asked her not to do the exact thing.

April slipped her hand into his, and he held it tightly as he made introduction after introduction after introduction to his new wife. Although he knew she was as wary as he was, April smiled gracefully through it all until everyone began to spread out and they were left alone.

He kissed the top of her head. "I had no idea this was being planned. I promise you that," he said against her upswept hair.

April smiled up at him. "Believe me, I know. Let's just grin and make the best of it."

With one last pull of her against his side with a strong arm, Lex and April moved into the living room to join their party.

They were immediately split up. Derrick led him onto the balcony.

"I don't know if I should start with you or War." Derrick handed Lex a glass of frothy beer.

Lex held the beer and slid his other hand into the pocket of his slacks. "How 'bout neither," he joked.

"War," Derrick said in decision. "Where the hell is he?"

Lex was determined to keep War's location private. If Derrick didn't know, then War—for whatever reason—didn't want him to know. "He's cool. I talked to him a few days ago."

"Next time you talk to him, tell him to call me."

Lex was actually surprised by the concern in Derrick's eyes. Of the bunch he was usually the brash and abrasive one. "I will."

"Okay, what's up with you being married—to a fine-ass woman by the way."

Lex looked through the French doors, his eyes searching for April. He found her standing by his mother and her sisters, Aunt June and Aunt Andell. She looked up suddenly as if she could feel his eyes on her and she smiled.

His heart literally flopped in his chest, and he winked at her in return.

"Word is you've known her for years?" Derrick asked with doubt.

Lex just took a sip of his beer as he eyed his friend over the rim of the glass.

"Then who's the chick you hooked up with in Vegas last week?" Derrick asked, looking cocky.

"I thought you gave up trial law," Lex asked.

Derrick looked from Lex to April. "You're right. I'll mind my business."

"Let's go in. I'm starving."

"Hey, Lex."

He turned to face Derrick.

"Your secret's safe with me," he said with a wink.

Lex just smiled and shook his head before raising his beer to his friend as they walked in.

"I mean, really, Candice, who is she?"

"Yes, she looks a hot mess."

"Certainly not what *I* expected for Alexander."

"I feel for you, dear. Imagine having a child eloping in this day and age."

"What of Tiffany?"

"It won't last...hopefully." Candice said clearly. "And as soon as it's over, Tiffany is all groomed to be the wife *I've* always wanted for him. I mean, April did not go to college. Can you imagine?"

The ladies, who were gathered in the kitchen, all laughed.

It took all the willpower April had not to walk into that kitchen and blow all those old biddies out of the water with a cursing-out they would never forget. Instead she took it as a wake-up call that this world—Lex's world—was not for her and the sooner she got back to *her* reality the better.

She turned from the kitchen but had made it only a few steps before she whirled around. F' it. There's more than one way to skin a cat.

The chattering stopped as soon as April walked into the kitchen. "Hello, ladies," she said with a big cheesy grin. "Since you were all talking about me behind my back I thought I'd give you a chance to be real and say it directly to me."

The ladies all looked shocked as April eyed each one.

"Really, April, behave. You're being overly sensitive and rude to my guests," Candice said, waving her hand in dismissal.

"*I'm* being rude?" April said in disbelief.

"Yes," Candice said with emphasis, forcing a smile as she saw the eyes shift between her and her daughter-in-law.

April eyed the women standing around the island. She turned to the one directly to her left. "You're Aunt Andell, right?"

The slender, silver-haired woman nodded.

"I hear when you were in your twenties you got thrown out of Spellman for sleeping with one of your professors."

"And, June, you were dealing with a married man for like ten years, right?"

"Lila, well we all know what happened to your daughter, Elizabeth. No need to rehash that. Although I've heard she gets the best of her moves from you."

"And, Dorice, I hear you and your reverend are doing more than praying when you're at the church with him all times of the night."

Each woman gasped in disapproval, horror or embarrassment. April smiled in satisfaction before she walked out of the kitchen.

"Oh, and Mama Macmillan? No more champagne for you up on the wagon."

April left them to ponder *that* as she went to find Lex. She made up every bit of it, but who cared. It was just what they deserved.

She looked everywhere and eventually found him out in the hallway with Tiffany. She was walking up just as the woman leaned in to kiss Lex. April's steps faltered. She got some satisfaction when he pushed Tiffany aside and reached in his pocket for a handkerchief to wipe his mouth.

"Tiffany, I'm sorry but I just don't see you that way. Please try to understand that."

"Yes, Tiffany, please do," April said, walking up to them.

Tiffany's lips thinned and blanched of color as she roughly brushed past April to enter the apartment.

Lex wiped the rest of the lipstick from his mouth. "Hey, you. This isn't what you—"

"It's none of my concern, Lex," April said, her words slashing off the rest of his.

He frowned. "What's wrong?"

"Nothing. Can we leave? I just want to go home...back to your place."

"April, we can't leave now. The party just started." He reached out to caress her shoulders, but April stepped back from him.

His face closed up. "Take the car if you want to go."

April walked to the elevator, punching the button with force. "Thanks for nothing."

Lex walked up to her. "April, baby, what's wrong? Let's go in for a little bit longer and I'll give you a nice rubdown when we get home."

April looked up at him. She didn't miss the heated once-over Lex gave her. "Don't even think about it."

"Oh, like you don't want it."

"You wish."

"I didn't have to wish last night or any other night we've spent together," he countered.

"If you're feeling horny call Tiffany. I'm sure she's more than willing to wet your whistle."

"I don't want Tiffany."

"If she's half the pro her friend is, you should have a ball."

"I want you."

"You want to have sex with me. There's a difference."

"Don't tell me what I want, April."

April met Lex's stare. "Somebody needs to tell you, because it's obvious you don't know what you want."

She walked past him to stride down the hall and through the door to the stairs.

She heard his footsteps behind her and whirled on the top step to face him. "What, Lex?"

"What do you mean by that?"

"You want me to stay in your apartment. You want me to cook for you. You want to hold my hand and whisper sweet nothings. You want to make love—"

"I don't deny anything you just said."

"But you don't want me for a wife."

Lex looked confused. "I thought we both wanted an annulment. So why am I the bad guy?"

April threw her hands up in frustration before she turned and stalked down the stairs. Halfway down she turned to look up at him. "Grow some balls and stop worrying about what people think or what they will say, and just be. Just live. Just do what you want to do," she said with conviction, her eyes filled with frustrated tears.

Lex's hand slashed the air. "Don't judge me, April. You don't know—"

"I know that you all set impossible standards and guidelines for each other based on preconceived hype of what's wrong and what's right. Maybe Elizabeth did what she did because she felt pressured to marry War. Maybe she never loved him but felt like she was supposed to love him. And marry him. And build a life with him."

Lex put his hands on his hips and dropped his head. "That's ridiculous, April. War and Elizabeth have been together forever. And what do they have to do with us?"

"Maybe their parents have been pushing them together forever." She locked her eyes with his as she climbed the stairs to stand before him. "Just like your precious mama wants you with Tiffany."

"Don't bring my mother into this." His eyes hardened and his voice was stone cold. "Furthermore you know nothing about Elizabeth and War."

"I know I saw Elizabeth's boyfriend and I asked why he did it. And he said, 'Because I thought she loved me.'" April took pleasure in the surprise she saw in Lex's eyes. "You people are so caught up in your own little world that's it like…to hell with anybody else that gets hurt along the way. Self-satisfaction is uppermost. Screw everyone else."

April turned, but Lex lightly grabbed her shoulders and turned her back to him to gather her into his arms. She brought both of her hands up between them and pushed hard against his chest. "Oh, no. It'll start with hugging. Then it's rubbing and kissing. Before you know we're humping like dogs right on the floor. Ain't gone happen, cap'n. People have feelings, and life is not always about what you want and what's convenient for you."

Lex released her, walked away and then walked back to her. "So you're saying that morning in Vegas when you woke up married to me you had no reservations? You had no fears? No regrets?"

April swallowed hard over a lump in her throat and shook her head. "I woke up thinking, wow, I am married to an incredible man. And I thought of that day as the first full day of the rest of our lives. So no. No regrets. No reservations. No fears. Or at least no more than any other newlywed."

Lex leaned against the wall. "So you're saying you want to stay married now?"

April held up her hands. "No, no, no, no, no. I am not trying to convince you to make this marriage work."

Lex wiped his face with one strong, broad hand.

April forced herself to calm down and she lowered her voice and softened her tone. "I would no more want you to stay with me, to please only me, than I like you living your life to please your parents. That would make me a hypocrite."

"So what do you want to do, April?" he asked, his voice resigned.

"I want out of this arrangement. I can't do it. Not anymore." April fought to keep the tears from falling as she looked up at him. "Tell them I cheated like Elizabeth. Tell them I wasn't as pretty and as smart as Tiffany. Tell them I don't know the difference between a damn salad fork and a dinner fork. Tell them whatever you want. Just sign the damn papers, Lex."

He shoved his hands in his pockets as he looked down at her. "You sure that's what you want?"

April nodded. "Yes, I'm sure."

Lex pushed off the wall and stepped down onto the same step with her. He wrapped his arms around her and kissed her softly and then deeply with uninhibited passion.

April's knees weakened, and she blinked rapidly to keep her tears from falling as she allowed herself one final kiss. She could feel the steam rise from the heat of their bodies as she stroked the fine hairs of his nape.

Their breathing was ragged and heavy as they stepped apart.

"Goodbye, April," he whispered against her still-parted lips.

"Goodbye."

Chapter 11

Never Never Gonna Give You Up
Two Months Later

April rose from the bed, frowning as a wave of nausea hit her. Feeling as if she would throw up, she raced to the bathroom, barely missing tripping over Clayton's feet as she did.

She felt light-headed and dropped to her knees by the commode, actually leaning on it.

"Ape, you okay? You don't sound so good."

She closed her eyes as dizziness hit her next.

"I don't feel too good. Must be some bad meat I had or something."

Clayton snorted. "Or some good meat. Some good *fertile* meat."

April retched several times before she vomited. She nearly buried her head inside the commode. And she stayed that way until she was sure it was over.

Clayton stepped into the bathroom as April struggled to flush the toilet. He filled a glass with water at the sink and wet a washcloth, handing her both.

April took them gladly, rising to her feet to rinse her mouth and then wipe her face. She frowned at her reflection in the mirror. "Lord, I look a mess."

When she turned to him in question, Clayton frowned a bit. "A true friend never lies."

April dropped the lid down on the commode and sat down on it heavily. "I've missed my last cycle," she admitted, releasing a heavy breath as she dropped her head into her hand.

Clayton rubbed her back reassuringly. "Brush your teeth and wipe your tears. Off to the doctor we go."

April nodded. "Call Gabby down here for

me. I want her to go with us." She rose to stand before the sink.

"No problem."

And she was left alone. Nothing but her and her reflection—and maybe a new little life who would be born with bluish-green eyes. Tears welled up. She dropped her head causing them to drop like raindrops into the sink.

It had been almost two months to the day since she kissed Lex goodbye for the last time in the stairwell of his parents' apartment building. Two long months since she'd seen him, held him or heard his voice.

And she missed him. She'd missed him as soon as she'd stepped out of his warm embrace that day. She'd missed him before she even finished walking down the stairwell away from him. Each step had made her miss him more.

And when she returned to the apartment alone, she allowed herself one last one walk-through of the place that felt like home to her. She had hugged Sterling close and made him promise to continue to take care of Lex for her. She had been touched by the hint of tears in his own eyes. They had been thick as thieves, and she would miss the elderly butler, as well.

Through it all she loved Lex. Even now she

knew he had forever claimed a permanent place in her heart and in her soul. Every day she fought to get over him. She fought and she failed.

And now this.

April looked at her soft belly and pressed a hand to it, amazed that a life might be growing inside of there. A life she created with Lex.

For the first time in a long time she smiled.

Lex loosened his tie and undid the top button of his shirt as he swiveled in his chair to look out at the magnificent view of the New York skyline. Usually it worked to calm him or to help him work out a strategy—be it personal or business.

Every day he became more and more dissatisfied with his life.

His intercom buzzed, and he reached over to press the button. "Yes?"

"Mr. Macmillan, Mr. Kinsey's here to see you."

Lex's spirits lifted. "Send him in." He sat up in his chair as his best friend strolled into his office. "What's the deal, War?"

"Nothing much. Nothing much." He unbuttoned his suit jacket as he sat in one of the club chairs before Lex's massive black-walnut desk.

"I was on my way to lunch and to play a few rounds at the club. You game?"

"I actually have nothing on my schedule for the rest of the afternoon." Lex stood.

"Um, I needed to talk to you first. That's why I really came by here," War said, leaning back in his chair to cross his ankle over his leg.

Lex sat back down. "Fire away."

"Remember how drunk we got after that wedding fiasco of mine?"

Lex nodded. "Do I? They poured me into bed."

"Do you remember telling me I should sue Elizabeth?"

Lex laughed until he saw how serious War's eyes were. "You're not kidding."

"Damn right I'm not." War rose from his chair to pace in front of Lex's desk. "We decided to pay for our wedding ourselves. Our little show of independence. Ever since I got back, all the bills have come to me. She hasn't paid for one single thing. Not even her dress."

Lex winced. "And it was a big wedding."

"A big wedding to help keep up the big front," War said dryly, moving back to take his chair.

Lex frowned. "What do you mean?"

"Elizabeth and I never had passion or that

kind of love you need to marry and spend the rest of your life with someone."

April's fiery words came back to him in a rush. *Maybe Elizabeth did what she did because she felt pressured to marry War. Maybe she never loved him but felt like she was supposed to love him. And marry him. And build a life with him.*

"Ever since I was old enough to remember, it's been Warrick and Elizabeth. We were together more out of the expectations of our parents than real love."

Exactly what April said.

Lex felt that familiar wave of sadness at the very thought of her. He tried his best to keep her out of his mind. Most of the time he succeeded. Other times he missed her so much that he literally ached.

"I never knew," Lex said, leaning his elbows on the top of his desk. "I thought you were the perfect couple."

"So did I until I carried my ass to Pennsylvania to lick my wounds." War wiped his mouth with his large hand. "I also realized I was more embarrassed than hurt by it."

"So this plan to sue Elizabeth isn't some misplaced anger at her cheating on you?" Lex asked, looking his friend straight in the eye.

War shook his head and looked indignant. "No, it's about some misplaced *bills,*" he said with comedic emphasis.

Lex laughed until tears were in his eyes.

Four Months Later

"Do you plan to tell him that you're pregnant?"

April looked over at her sister as they lounged by the fireplace drinking hot chocolate and browsing through fashion magazines. "I didn't say that I wasn't going to tell him, Gabby. I don't plan to turn my life into any more of a *Lifetime* movie than it already is."

Gabby nodded and shifted from laying on her belly to sitting with her back pressed to the sofa. "Okay. So *when* are you going to tell him that he has a son on the way?"

April's hand went to her stomach. "What's the rush? The baby isn't due for another three months."

Gabby frowned and then ran her fingers through her now shoulder-length auburn hair. She opened her mouth and then closed it as if she stopped herself from saying something. "Girl," she began, and then stopped, held up her hand and closed her eyes.

April knew her sister was counting to ten.

"I'm afraid, okay? I said it. Stop counting."

Gabby popped one eye opened and smiled. "I was praying not counting. And see...it worked."

April smiled with her. "I know it works. Remember I had to pray for the Lord to give you a life, and now you have a good marriage and a beautiful baby. Thank me whenever you're ready."

Instead Gabby tossed a soft throw pillow at her.

"Okay, what are you afraid of?" she asked, stretching her legs out in front of her.

"Afraid? Who's afraid?" Addie asked as she walked into the living room pushing the baby carriage.

"Ape's afraid to tell Mr. Manhattan—"

"Lex," April stressed.

"Lex, then. She's afraid to tell Lex she's pregnant," Gabby said, moving to rise.

"First, Gabby, sit right on down. That baby is sleeping and minding his own business, so leave him be 'fore he's more spoiled than he is now." Addie's tone was no-nonsense. She turned to April. "You need to call your baby daddy and stop frontin'."

"I thought y'all blocked the video channels on the cable in her room." April muttered out the side of her mouth to Gabby.

Addie made her classic Aunt Esther from *Good Times* face. April blew her a kiss.

"What are you afraid of?" Gabby asked, reaching for her cup to sip her hot chocolate.

"That I'll wind up killing him because he'll be disappointed when I tell him."

Gabby shook her head in shame while Addie threw her hands up in the air.

"Why do you always see the glass half-empty?" Gabby asked, setting aside the *Vibe Vixen* magazine she just finished reading.

"Same reason you do," April returned.

"Ain't that the truth," Addie added.

Gabby looked at them both. "When did this become about me?"

"You are all over me to tell Lex, but it took you six years to tell Max you liked him."

"Like him?" Addie snorted as she looked down at the baby sleeping in the carriage. "Try love-her-some him."

Gabby ignored Addie. "Yes, but once you helped me—like I'm trying to do for you—once you helped me to see I should walk out on faith—"

"Try she's was one step from stalking," Addie added in the background with a little chuckle.

"Look at the love I was rewarded with," Gabby said raising her voice to talk over Addie.

"Humph. 'Round here half-out-her-mind loving Max till she dressed down so no other man would notice her." Addie closed her eyes and rocked back and forth while she raised her hand like she was in church. "Let the church say amen....a-men."

April and Gabby looked over at Addic.

"Thank you, Addie. We get the point," Gabby said with emphasis.

"I know your coodymama singing hallelujah."

"Addie, please!"

The older woman picked the baby out of the carriage to lay across her lap as she changed his diaper.

That was Addie, and she was the same all the time.

Gabby scooted across the floor to grab her sister's hand. "You gave me the nudge to be honest with Max about my feelings. Now I want you to be honest with Lex about this baby."

April took her sister's hand and pressed it to her round abdomen. "The baby kicked," she said in reverence.

"Oh," Gabby sighed, as she felt the movement against her palm.

"Bet your baby daddy wanna feel it, too. *If* he knew. Humph," Addie threw into the mix.

"I'm going to tell him." April looked at Gabby and Addie and found both their faces filled with disbelief. "I am."

Just as soon as I work up the nerve.

One Month Later

"I am worried sick about Alexander, Harris," Candice said to her husband as they rode in their limo. "First that ridiculous marriage to that April girl and now this."

Big Mac looked out the window at the passing metropolitan landscape. He was busy trying to block out his wife and troubleshoot this latest sudden move in his son's life.

"How are we going to handle this, Harris?" she asked. "We have got to gain control of this situation before Alexander really gets out of hand."

Harris nearly bit the end off the unlit cigar he held in his mouth.

"And, Harris, do not light that cigar. You know I cannot stand the smell of those awful disgusting—"

"Be quiet, Candice," he bit out, frustrated beyond belief with his wife.

Candice turned in the limo seat to stare at him. "What did you say?" she asked sharply.

Big Mac turned on his seat to face her, as well. "I *said* to be quiet."

"How dare—"

He held up one beefy hand. "No, let me speak, for a change. You want to run everyone's damn life, and enough is enough. If your meddling has pushed my son—"

"*Your* son?"

"Damn right, *my* son, because you seem to forget that I have just as much say-so in his life as you do, and right now neither one of us should have so much to say."

"Harris," Candice said in surprise, tears brimming in her eyes. "Why are you talking to me this way?"

"Because enough is enough," he said firmly, reaching over to gather her hands into his. "When I was working twenty hours a day, I let you take over control of this family, and I see now that I was wrong. You have got to calm down with *your* opinions. *Your* beliefs. *Your* wishes. Life is not all about you, Candice. Yes,

Candice, believe it or not some people don't care about your opinion on everything."

A tear fell, and she turned her head away from him.

Big Mac raised his hand to lightly turn her face back to him. "I love you. I really do, but I will not let anyone—not even you—run my son out of my life."

"I love Alexander," she insisted, allowing him to pull her against his chest.

"I know you do, but you got to let him make his own choices and so do I." Big Mac stroked her hair and was surprised when his wife didn't reprimand him for ruining her hairdo. It felt good to hold her.

"I pushed that company on him and never once asked if he wanted it," he said honestly with a desire to ease some of the harshness in his judgment of her.

"I only did what was best," she said, her words muffled against his chest as her bejeweled hands clutched his lapel.

"No, be honest, Candice. You did what *you* thought was right and to hell with anyone who didn't agree with you."

"*Maybe* you're right."

Big Mac kissed the top of Candice's head. "All right, now fix your face and let's go talk to our son."

Lex's intercom buzzed.

He leaned forward to push the button. "Yes?"

"Your parents are on their way in."

"Thank you."

The door opened and his parents stepped inside.

Lex rose to come around his desk and kiss his mother's upturned cheek and to shake his father's hand. "How are you both feeling?" he asked, sitting down on the edge of his desk before them.

"I was feeling fine until you—"

"Candice," Big Mac said a bit sternly as he reached out to lightly clasp his hands over hers.

Lex's eyes dropped to take in the gesture, and he was amazed when his mother closed her mouth, offering no protest.

"Son, your decision to take an immediate leave of absence caught us both off guard."

"As my executive vice president, Arthur Miller, is more than capable to serve as acting CEO in my absence," Lex explained as he rose and walked over to the minifridge in the corner to pull out a bottle of water. "It's only for six months."

"But why, Alexander?" Candice asked. "Is something wrong?"

Lex took a sip of his water as he sat behind his desk. "No, Mother, nothing's wrong…anymore."

Candice and Big Mac shared a look before turning to look at him.

"I want to start to have the kind of relationship where we can be open and honest with each other about everything. No judgment. No criticism."

Candice clutched Big Mac's hands tighter as she stared at her son. "Alexander—"

"Let the boy speak, Candy."

"Actually, Dad, that's the thing. I'm a man, not a boy." Lex set the water bottle down and leaned forward to prop his elbows atop his desk. "And it's time I step up like a man and give you both some truths about me."

Candice's knuckles nearly whitened as she clutched her husband's hand even tighter.

"I appreciate the opportunities you both have afforded me. It made my life easier and I understand and appreciate that…but I am tired of feeling like I owe you control over every aspect of my life because of it."

"That was never our intention, Alexander," Candice said, sadness obvious in her eyes.

"Trust me to run my personal life the same way you have entrusted me to run this corporation. And trust me, my personal life is a whole lot simpler." Lex smiled at them. "I want to be able to share my life—my real life—with you. I'm tired of giving you the facade that you want, instead of the real son that you have and should love and respect regardless."

Lex paused, giving them a moment to digest that, because the best was yet to come.

"Eventually I want to be able to sit you both down and introduce you to the real Alexander Macmillan, but I am a little pressed for time today." Lex rose and pulled on his suit jacket. "*But* I will admit that I love April and I dishonored her and our love by lying to you about our relationship."

Lex held up his hand when they started to speak.

"I lucked out," he told them with honesty as he packed his briefcase. "I was blessed to find my Mrs. Right and know it immediately. Enough to marry her after just a week of being with her."

Candice gasped and literally clutched her pills. Big Mac frowned a bit.

"No judgment. No criticism," he reminded them as he slid his airline tickets into the breast pocket of his suit. "I was lucky enough to experience love at first sight and I turned my back on it. I put everyone else's thoughts and feelings above what I knew I felt and what I knew I wanted. People I don't know even know. And now I refuse to deny myself any longer."

He grabbed his briefcase by the handle, lifting it from the desk as he strode to the door.

Big Mac and Candice jumped to their feet, turning to face him. "Where are you going?" Big Mac asked.

Lex pulled the door to his office open and looked over his shoulder with a smile—a real smile.

"April's pregnant. I'm going to bring my family home, and I'm not leaving Richmond until I do just that."

Without another look back Lex walked out of the office.

There was plenty of hustle and bustle around Max and Gabby's estate as Simone Love, celebrity event planner, and her crew made the final preparations for the baby shower.

April held her belly as she looked out the bay window as balloons and ribbons in pearlized shades of lime, pink, peach and yellow were floated in the air. There was a carnival theme cake with a harlequin design in the same colors. April thought that so appropriate since it reminded her of the colorful tented ceiling of Le Cirque, the restaurant where she had her first date with Lex.

Lex.

She would give everything she had plus take out a loan to have him be part of the pregnancy. So many times she had held the phone in her hands and hadn't found the strength to call him and tell him. "Well, little Alexander, just four weeks to go," she said softly.

"So, our son will have my name?"

April whirled around as fast as she could and gasped as Lex walked into the kitchen with a brightly wrapped present in his hands.

Her eyes devoured him. Remembered him. Nothing about him had changed. He was as familiar as her love for him. "Lex?" she said, emotions already swelling up inside of her.

Get right, April. Come on now. Get right.

"Who told you?" she asked accusingly.

Lex stopped beside the island and sat his gift on it before he slid both his hands into the pockets of his loose fitting khakis. "Your sister, but that's not important, Ape, you should have told me."

April moved to the other side of the island, putting it between them. "I was going to tell you. I would have never kept your child from you. I just needed time."

Lex nodded as his eyes scanned her face. "You look beautiful, April," he said huskily, his face serious and intense.

April's heart hammered in her chest as she gripped the edges of the island. "Thank you."

"Are you okay? Is everything okay with the baby?" he asked, his eyes dropping down to her rotund belly.

April nodded as she bit her bottom lip. "Why are you here, Lex?"

"Because I love you," he said without hesitation as he locked those mesmerizing eyes with hers.

April felt breathless at his words. "Don't tell me that now because I'm pregnant, Alexander Macmillan."

Lex had just a hint of a smile at his supple

lips as he looked over at her. "Don't pretend that's the first time I told you I loved you."

April felt and looked completely stunned.

April, I love your ass. I do. I love you.

Lex nodded and smiled at the look in her eyes. "I know you remember. I was drunk that night, but not crazy."

April shook her head, closing her eyes as she held up her hand. "What...what is ...what—"

"I told my parents how we really met," Lex said, moving around the island to come closer to her.

Again she felt shock, and it showed.

"I told them that I love you and I have loved you from that first night we spent together."

April's breaths came in short spurts as if she was hyperventilating. She felt herself backing away from him even as she felt like running to him. Could it be? Did Lex love her just as much as she loved him?

"I told them I wasn't coming back unless I brought my family with me, April Macmillan."

"No, no, no, no," she said with emphasis, looking up at him with tear-filled eyes. "I'm not April Macmillan anymore, remember?"

Lex leaned across the island for the gift and gently pushed it toward her. "Open it," he urged in a deep husky timbre that made her weak at the knees.

April shook her head.

Lex pulled the package back to him and tore the colorful paper to lift the lid from the box. His eyes stay locked on her as he turned the box over.

Hundreds—maybe thousands—of shredded strips of paper dropped onto the island like confetti.

April's eyes searched his.

"Our annulment papers," he said, answering the unspoken question. "I never filed the papers, April. I *never*...filed...the papers."

April clutched the island for support. She wondered about that but just assumed it took time. She bit her bottom lip to keep it from quivering. She smiled a little and he smiled in return.

"You love me," she stated without question.

"Yes, baby, I love you."

"You're happy about the baby."

"More than you know."

"You came to take us home."

"Damn right."

April let the tears flow as Lex took two large steps forward to clasp her face with his hands and kiss the tears from her face with loving tenderness.

She lifted her hands to caress his sides. "I love you," she told him with emotion just before his mouth lowered to hers with heat, intensity and much love.

Epilogue

You and I
Ten Years Later

"You're as beautiful a bride today as you were ten years ago, Mrs. Macmillan," Lex whispered into April's ear as they danced to the soft strains of the R & B classic "You and I."

She leaned back in his embrace to look up into those eyes. "You ain't looking half-bad yourself, Mr. Macmillan."

Lex pressed her closer. "I can't wait for the honeymoon."

"Really?" she asked with a purr.

He nodded. "I want you to do your little trick with your muscles for me. It's been a while."

She flung her head back and laughed, just as Lex dipped her almost to the floor before bringing her back up to kiss her lips with a smile. "Your wish is my command."

Lex wiggled his brows. "I'm going to hold you to that."

April truly felt blessed. What started as a week-long affair in Vegas turned into the love of her life. And they were in love—deeply so. And their life was good.

Never had April guessed she would have three sons—her boys, Alex, Jr., Harrison and Mikell. She loved them to death, and although she wanted to give them the world, she fought hard to ensure their grandparents didn't spoil them or set them up with silver spoons. And she knew her husband was proud that he had the kind of honest and open relationship with his sons that he never had growing up with his own parents.

It took time, but eventually Lex did have a better relationship with his parents. Not perfect but better.

April's eyes happened to light on her mother-in-law standing near the edge of the dance floor talking to Addie. She would love to have been a fly on the wall for that conversation.

In the morning they all were leaving for Disneyland. Their boys. Max and Gabby and their own three children. Addie. Clayton and his "husband" Raoul with their adopted daughter. Even Mr. and Mrs. Macmillan.

Were they crazy to take their unique family along for their honeymoon?

Lex had wanted to send the kids to Max and Gabby while they traveled to Paris for two weeks, but April instead asked for a family trip. He surprised her with the news just this morning before the ceremony to renew their vows.

But that was Lex. He wasn't perfect, but he was perfect for her. In ten years he had proven to be everything she ever wanted in man. Never once since their reconciliation had she felt like she couldn't count on him or their marriage.

They were one of the lucky ones.

April leaned back in his arms and looked up at her husband. "I love you so much," she told him huskily.

"And I love you just the same."

"Mama. Daddy. We wanna dance."

They shared one kiss before their sons pushed in between them.

April smiled with love as the five of them joined hands and began to dance together.

About the Author

Niobia Simone Bryant is the nationally bestselling and award-winning author of eight works of romance fiction.

She lives in South Carolina with her boyfriend and is busy at work completing a mainstream novel and starting her next romance novel.

For more on this author go to her Web site: www.geocities.com/niobia_bryant, where you can join her free online book club, Niobia Bryant News. Also feel free to e-mail her: niobia_bryant@yahoo.com.

Dear Reader

Yet another story of love and passion that we have shared together. Sassy April Dutton from *Can't Get Next to You* has finally found a love all her own after years and years of what she and her sister, Gabrielle, call "man drama." And don't we all have stories to tell, to burn, to bury and then to forget (smile).

I loved the idea of one of those quickie Vegas weddings actually working out, and I thought the storyline was just right for April—just like Lex was just right for her as well.

Thank you times a thousand for all your wonderful support over the years for my books, my characters and my stories filled with "Soul Love."

Love 2 Live & Live 2 Love.

Blessings 2 U,

N.

KIMANI
FORGED OF STEELE
The sizzling miniseries from
USA TODAY bestselling author
BRENDA JACKSON
Sebastian Steele's takeover of
Jocelyn Mason's fledgling company
topples when Jocelyn takes over
Sebastian's heart
NIGHT HEAT
AVAILABLE SEPTEMBER 2006
FROM KIMANI™ ROMANCE
Love's Ultimate Destination
AVAILABLE JANUARY 2007
BEYOND TEMPTATION
Available at your favorite retail outlet.
Visit Kimani Romance at www.kimanipress.com.
KRBJNHR